## They had guns!

Both men in the speedboat pulled bandannas over the lower half of their faces, and one of the men hefted a rifle to his shoulder, aiming the weapon at Tessa.

Jeff grabbed his sidearm. "Tessa! Get down!"

A startling bang followed by an even louder pop jolted through Tessa. One side of the Zodiac deflated like a balloon pricked by a needle. She was being shot at!

Jeff jumped over the still-inflated side of the Zodiac and dropped down beside her on his back, his gun in front of him, aimed toward the lake. "You okay?"

"Yes. You?" He fired off two rounds. The deafening noise reverberated inside her head.

The speedboat roared away. They were leaving. Relief made her melt into the floor.

Jeff jumped to his feet and tugged on her arm. "They're circling back. Get up. We have to run for the trees."

Galvanized by fear and adrenaline, she scrambled out of the boat and followed Jeff.

## Books by Terri Reed

### Love Inspired Suspense

*Double Deception
 Beloved Enemy
 Her Christmas Protector
*Double Jeopardy
*Double Cross
*Double Threat Christmas
 Her Last Chance
 Chasing Shadows
 Covert Pursuit
 Holiday Havoc
   "Yuletide Sanctuary"
 Daughter of Texas
†The Innocent Witness
†The Secret Heiress
 The Deputy's Duty
†The Doctor's Defender
†The Cowboy Target

Scent of Danger
Texas K-9 Unit Christmas
 "Rescuing Christmas"
Treacherous Slopes
Undercover Marriage
**Danger at the Border

*The McClains
†Protection Specialists
**Northern Border Patrol

### Love Inspired

Love Comes Home
A Sheltering Love
A Sheltering Heart
A Time of Hope
Giving Thanks for Baby
Treasure Creek Dad

## TERRI REED

At an early age Terri Reed discovered the wonderful world of fiction and declared she would one day write a book. Now she is fulfilling that dream and enjoys writing for Love Inspired Books. Her second book, *A Sheltering Love,* was a 2006 RITA® Award finalist and a 2005 National Readers' Choice Award finalist. Her book *Strictly Confidential,* book five in the Faith at the Crossroads continuity series, took third place in the 2007 American Christian Fiction Writers Book of the Year Award, and *Her Christmas Protector* took third place in 2008. She is an active member of both Romance Writers of America and American Christian Fiction Writers. She resides in the Pacific Northwest with her college-sweetheart husband, two wonderful children and an array of critters. When not writing, she enjoys spending time with her family and friends, gardening and playing with her dogs.

You can write to Terri at P.O. Box 19555, Portland, OR 97280. Visit her on the web at www.loveinspiredauthors.com, leave comments on her blog, www.ladiesofsuspense.blogspot.com, or email her at terrireed@sterling.net.

# DANGER AT THE BORDER

## TERRI REED

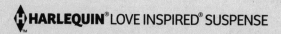
HARLEQUIN® LOVE INSPIRED® SUSPENSE

Recycling programs
for this product may
not exist in your area.

LOVE INSPIRED BOOKS

ISBN-13: 978-0-373-67629-3

DANGER AT THE BORDER

Copyright © 2014 by Terri Reed

All rights reserved. Except for use in any review, the reproduction
or utilization of this work in whole or in part in any form by any
electronic, mechanical or other means, now known or hereinafter
invented, including xerography, photocopying and recording, or in
any information storage or retrieval system, is forbidden without
the written permission of the editorial office, Love Inspired Books,
233 Broadway, New York, NY 10279 U.S.A.

This is a work of fiction. Names, characters, places and incidents are
either the product of the author's imagination or are used fictitiously, and
any resemblance to actual persons, living or dead, business establishments,
events or locales is entirely coincidental.

This edition published by arrangement with Love Inspired Books.

® and TM are trademarks of Love Inspired Books, used under license.
Trademarks indicated with ® are registered in the United States Patent
and Trademark Office, the Canadian Intellectual Property Office and in
other countries.

www.Harlequin.com

Printed in U.S.A.

Our soul waits for the Lord:
He is our help and our shield.
—*Psalms* 33:20

To Teal and Kim,
I couldn't have asked for better sisters.

# ONE

"Thank you, Randy." Biologist Dr. Tessa Cleary smiled at the young ranger sitting in the driver's seat of the Forest Service truck.

"Sure thing, Doc." He saluted her with a grin crinkling his tanned face.

Randy had picked her up from the airport in Bellingham, Washington, and driven her on the long, windy road to the ranger station at Glen Lake in the North Cascades National Forest. At least five years younger than her twenty-eight years, Randy had kept up a running dialogue on the lake and the human inhabitants who made the forest their home. He obviously knew the area well.

Tessa had been content to listen but was glad to reach her destination and escape the confines of the truck cab. The smell of tobacco coming off the young ranger had been overpowering, even with the window down. A little queasy, she climbed from the vehicle and stretched. However, the agitated churning of her tummy wasn't due to motion sickness, but from the recent reports of fish kills and the outburst of breathing problems swimmers in Glen Lake had been experiencing.

Shielding her eyes against the late-summer sun, she surveyed her surroundings and filled her lungs with the sweet scent of fresh mountain air. Tall conifers dominated the forest, but she detected many deciduous trees surrounding the sparkling shores of the reservoir lake, as well.

A hidden paradise. One to be enjoyed by those willing to venture to the middle of the Pacific Northwest.

The lake should be filled with boats and swimmers, laughing children, fishing poles and water skis.

But all was still.

Silent.

The seemingly benign water was filled

with something toxic harming both the wild-life and humans.

Her office had received a distressing call yesterday that dead trout had washed ashore on the lake, and recreational swimmers were presenting with respiratory distress after swimming in the lake.

As a field biologist for the USDA Forest Service's Fish and Aquatic Ecology Unit, her job was to determine what exactly that *something* was as quickly as possible and stop it.

She'd convinced her boss she couldn't wait for a team to be assembled. She needed to get to Glen Lake ASAP. The team would follow but not for another forty-eight hours. She'd hopped on the next available flight from Logan, Utah, to the state of Washington to as-sess the reports of contamination in the water.

A wet, hot tongue licked her hand. Startled, she jerked back. A large Rottweiler stared up at her.

"Ooh, aren't you a beauty?" she cooed and scratched the dog behind the ear.

"Here she is!" A booming voice full of anticipation rang out. The dog trotted away, apparently losing interest in her as she turned her attention to the ranger station.

The building, like many she'd visited around the country, had a peaked roofline to keep winter elements from accumulating, and natural wood and material painted in earthy tones to help the structure blend in with the environment.

A mixed group of civilians and uniformed personnel gathered on the wide wooden porch.

She recognized the park ranger by his tan uniform. She figured the man in the dark brown uniform with the gold-star badge was the Okanagan County sheriff.

All eyes were trained on her. All except one man's.

Tall with dark hair, he stood in profile talking to the sheriff. Too many people blocked him from full view for her to see an agency logo on his forest-green uniform. Probably from EPA. She'd worked with agents from the Environmental Protection Agency on other cases, though she thought their uniforms were dark colored. Either way, she hoped this didn't turn into a power struggle.

The ranger, a lanky man in his sixties, and a woman of the same age dressed in jeans and a plaid shirt broke away from the crowd to hurry down the stairs toward her.

Tessa forced a composed smile, though inside she was anxious to get going. The longer they waited, the more damage to the lake and its inhabitants there would be, but she knew in situations like this it was best to appear confident and calm. Showing any sign of concern would create panic.

She didn't want anyone to freak out. At least, not until she knew what they were dealing with. There could be any number of reasons for the fish kills—the most common causes were oxygen depletion, algae, disease or pollution.

Only the last two could explain the swimmers' breathing issues.

The ranger approached with his hand out. "You must be Dr. Cleary. I'm Ranger George Harris, and this is my wife, Ellen. Thank you for coming so quickly."

"I got here as soon as I could," she said, shaking each of their outstretched hands.

"I did as you asked," George said. "All

boating activity and swimming in the lake has ceased. The sheriff has officers stationed at the docks to make sure no one takes any watercrafts out."

"Good," she said. "It would be best for everyone to stay out of the lake until we know what's going on."

"You're going to find the cause?" An older man stalked forward, the Rottweiler at his heels. His bushy eyebrows lowered over dark eyes. "You're just a scrawny lady. What can you possibly do?" He threw his hands in the air. "We're doomed."

Not letting his words affect her took effort. This wasn't the first time she'd been dismissed before being given a chance. She'd hoped her career would be the one place where she'd be accepted for who she was. Unfortunately, that was a fight she constantly found herself battling.

But at least she had knowledge and expertise to back her up. "Sir, I assure you I know what I'm doing. I will get to the bottom of what's going on."

The old man harrumphed.

Ellen stepped forward and placed a hand

on the old man's arm. "Henry, enough with the dramatics." She turned to Tessa. "As you can probably understand, folks around here are pretty upset. The resort at the southern tip of the lake has people bailing on their reservations right and left. The other small communities along the shoreline are suffering, as well."

"Without the tourist trade, my business will die. I'll have to sell." Henry's fists tightened at his sides. "Where am I going to go? Huh?"

Ellen patted his arm. "It won't come to that."

Tessa turned her attention to Ranger Harris. "Do you have any idea where the contamination is originating?"

He shook his head. "We haven't come across the source. At least not on our side of the lake. I'm not sure what's happening across the border." George ran a hand through his graying hair as his gaze strayed to the lake. "Whatever this is, it isn't coming from our side."

"Let's not go casting aspersions on our friends to the north until we know more. Okay, George?"

The deep baritone voice came from Tessa's right. She turned to find herself confronted by a set of midnight-blue eyes filled with curiosity.

She blinked at the attractive man towering over her. Answering curiosity rose within her. Who was he? And why was he here? She couldn't drag her gaze away from his face to check his uniform.

His gaze slid the length of her, burning a trail over her plaid shirt, jeans and work boots, and back to her eyes. She drew herself up to her full height, though she only managed to reach his shoulders, refusing to squirm beneath his perusal.

However, she was glad she'd corralled her wild curls with a clip and had applied some lip gloss when her plane landed.

She mentally scoffed. Not that she cared a whit what this man thought of her. Doing her job wasn't dependent on meeting his approval.

His well-formed lips curved upward slightly, sending a shiver gallivanting across her flesh. But she held his gaze, unwilling to let him think he could intimidate or embarrass her, despite the heat creeping up her neck.

George cleared his throat. "Dr. Cleary, this is Agent Steele with the U.S. Customs and Border Protection service."

Ah. That explained his presence. Finally able to tear her gaze from his, she noted his gold badge with the unmistakable bald eagle perched at the top with its wings spread as if in flight. Considering the lake crossed the international border separating the U.S. and Canada, she wasn't surprised that a Border Patrol agent had been called.

Since 9/11, the U.S. and Canadian governments had upped the amount of personnel and security measures along its shared boundary. The forestland on both sides of the line, though rugged terrain, had seen its share of attempted illegal crossings.

"Jeff," Agent Steele said, holding out his hand.

She hesitated a fraction before slipping her hand into his. "Tessa."

His big, warm palm pressed against hers like a shock pad, sending waves of sensation up her arm.

She extracted her hand quickly and curled her fingers to disperse the disturbing reaction. Basic biology at work here. Nothing more. Just because the guy looked as if he belonged on a billboard ad rather than out in the middle of a forest didn't mean she had to get all goofy about him. She wasn't in the market for a romance. The last time she'd allowed the rush of attraction to rule, she'd ended up busted to pieces when the relationship took a nosedive like the pH level in an aquarium when exposed to too much $CO_2$.

The gleam in his eyes made her think he'd noticed her reaction to him. She resisted the urge to put her hand to her warm cheeks. No sense in confirming her initial attraction.

"I look forward to working with you."

His smooth-as-silk voice wrapped around her. It took a moment for his words to process. "Working with me?"

She couldn't imagine what he could do to help her or the work she did. He'd only be a nuisance. A distraction she didn't want.

Instead of answering, he gestured to the man beside him. "This is Sheriff Larkin."

Tessa jerked her gaze from the too-handsome Agent Steele to acknowledge the sheriff with a handshake. "Sheriff."

"We're counting on you to deal with this," the sheriff said.

"Have there been any fires in the area recently? The contamination could be chemicals used in firefighting that seeped into the soil or into the water."

Sheriff Larkin shook his head. "No. Not for a couple of years."

So much for that theory. "I'll need to test samples of the water and the soil along the lakeshore on both sides."

"I'll have a boat ready to take you wherever you need to go," Ranger Harris promised.

"You have the fish samples?" She'd asked that they collect as many different samples as possible from various points along the lakeshore. That way she would have a better chance of figuring out if the contamination was widespread or localized to a specific section.

"Yes. I have at least two dozen waiting for you."

Anxiety spurted through her. She was

careful to keep her voice even. "Two dozen dead fish?"

"Yes, ma'am," George stated. "From up and down both sides of the lake all the way to the borderline. Each is labeled where on the lake it came from, like you'd asked."

Her stomach sank. So much for hoping the contaminant was limited and hadn't had a chance to cover too large a portion of the lake or to settle in the sediment. With that many dead trout turning up, the toxin had spread.

She looked at Agent Steele—Jeff. "You'll need to alert the Canadian authorities that the lake is contaminated."

Agent Steele exchanged a glance with the sheriff. "We've communicated to the Canadians that there is an issue with the lake water. They are taking appropriate precautions."

"Could an oil or gasoline spill cause the fish to die?" Ellen asked.

"And swimmers to get sick?" George added.

Tessa shifted her gaze to the older couple. "Has anyone reported a spill?"

George shook his head.

"I doubt a tourist would report an accident

like that. Too eager to save their own bacon than protect the water," Henry shot out.

"What happens if it is a spill?" Ellen asked.

"We'd skim the spill from the surface by using a boom or skimmer device that sucks up the contaminant." Cleaning up even a small portion of the lake wouldn't be an easy task, but it would be doable.

Jeff's intense gaze held hers. "And if it's not oil or gas? How do we clean it up?"

"If the pollutant has settled into the sediment, then dredging will be necessary."

"How long will that take?" George asked.

Looking at the lake, she said, "I don't have a definitive answer."

"Your best guess?" the sheriff interjected.

"I don't make guesses," she said.

"Try," Jeff prodded.

The weight of his stare pried the words from her. "Considering the size and depth of the lake, maybe a week or two. Maybe more."

George groaned.

"Summer's not over yet. We still have several weeks of good weather. We can't afford to lose the tourism," Ellen said, distress ringing in her tone.

"See, I told you, we're doomed!" Henry interjected in a loud roar.

Tessa held up a hand. "I won't know what to do or what we're dealing with until I locate the toxin and assess the damage."

"What do we do first?" Jeff asked, his intense gaze drilling into her.

"*We* don't do anything." Tessa hoped he understood where the boundary line lay. She didn't need him getting in her way. She turned to Ranger Harris. "I need to examine the fish."

Jeff tapped his foot against the linoleum floor of the Glen Lake ranger station as he talked on his cell phone. He stood in the hallway outside the room where the "fish doctor" was doing her thing. Overhead, the fluorescent lights hummed, loud enough to make it difficult to hear the man speaking on the other end of the phone. Jeff's blood pressure ratcheted skyward. The summer heat invaded the rangers' break room, making him sweat. He tugged at the collar of his uniform shirt.

"We can't let this turn into an international disaster." Deputy Director Darrin Moore's deep voice held an intense tone that never failed to make Jeff think of his father in lecture mode. But for some reason, Jeff accepted his boss's instruction better than his father's. "Contain the situation, Agent Steele. Determine if this is an accident or an attack."

Jeff detected the note of concern underlying Moore's words. "Are you suggesting this could be an act of terrorism?"

"I'm erring on the side of caution." The deputy director was as buttoned-down as they came. All of the men and women Jeff had met from Homeland Security headquarters were the epitome of professional.

Protecting the great nation of the United States was serious business.

And tough. For all Homeland Security and Border Patrol agents.

The nation's security was more than a job. At least to Jeff.

Stationed at the port of entry in Blaine, Washington, Jeff worked to keep the northern border between the U.S. and Canada safe from threats against the American and Canadian people. He'd been honored when his boss tagged him to be a part of the IBETS—Integrated Border Enforcement Teams, a binational task force working to enhance border integrity and security along the shared U.S./ Canada line.

The deputy director had told him yesterday to hustle to Glen Lake. Jeff had complied without hesitation. When he'd arrived at the Glen Lake ranger station a few hours ago, he'd found frightened people wanting answers.

He prayed the woman in the next room would provide them.

"Dr. Cleary's dissecting the dead fish as we speak," Jeff explained to Deputy Director Moore. "We'll have answers shortly."

At least Jeff hoped so. Tessa seemed like the type of person who worked methodically and efficiently. She'd certainly turned out to be a surprise.

He wasn't sure what he'd expected. Someone older, earthier, less curvy.

Instead, Tessa Cleary, with her striking auburn hair, liquid-amber-colored eyes and smattering of freckles crossing the bridge of her pert nose, was trouble with a capital *T*. He knew her type. He'd dated his fair share of them.

Smart—the woman was a Ph.D.—bossy and demanding. High maintenance.

He could almost hear the sputtering that would happen when Tessa saw the accommodations. The cabins on the edge of the lake used for the Forest Service were barely a step up from a tent.

He'd hazard a guess the doctor's idea of roughing it was not having reservations.

Hmm. Okay, they could have that in common. He didn't particularly like sleeping on the ground or a saggy cot but certainly would if needed.

He'd noticed there was no gold band or tan line suggesting a ring recently had graced her slender hand. Not that her marital status was any of his business. He didn't do commitment because commitment equaled heartache, a state of being he'd rather not experience again.

"Call once you have the doctor's findings," Moore said before hanging up.

Jeff walked into the makeshift autopsy room.

The aroma of vanilla from lit candles underscored the decaying-fish stink.

Stopping in the doorway, he watched Tessa. Her hands were steady, quick and efficient as she sliced and diced. She'd already worked her way through one tray and had started on another.

She placed a sample on the slide for the microscope and moved forward to peer into the eyepiece. Her red hair stuck out the back of the hairnet, the tarnished strands vibrant against her green tartan-patterned shirt. With appreciation, his gaze lingered over her trim waist, nice curves and long, lean legs.

She straightened and made some notes on the pad of paper at her side. She froze and then whipped around to stare at him.

"How long have you been standing there?" Her voice vibrated with indignation.

"A few seconds." He stepped fully into the room. "Did you figure out what killed the fish?" Anticipation knotted his gut.

"Yes and no." She stripped off her rubber gloves and tossed them in a wastebasket. "It wasn't a spill of oil or gasoline."

Dread tightened the muscles in his shoulders. "So then, what? Natural causes?" He could only hope.

She slanted him a sharp glance. "Hardly. The damage done to these poor fish is indicative of a chemical agent."

Jeff's stomach dropped. "What sort of chemical?"

"I won't know until I send tissue, water and soil samples out for analysis."

"How long will that take?"

"If the lab can rush, I should have the findings by the end of the week."

Running his palm over his jaw, Jeff said, "Any chance a chemical could have accidentally polluted the water?"

She undid her hairnet, letting her auburn tresses fall around her shoulders. His gaze was drawn to the burnished curls.

"I need to find the source, then I'll know," she said,

He dragged his gaze from her pretty hair and met her gaze. "George has a boat ready for us."

Her copper-colored eyebrows rose. "You are not accompanying me."

"But I am." He didn't wait for her to argue. He cupped her elbow to propel her toward the door. "My job is to protect this country. I need your help to do it."

"Wait! My bag!" She jerked out of his grasp and hurriedly packed up her equipment.

"I'll get it." He reached for the strap. She sidestepped him and marched out the door.

Shaking his head at her stubbornness, he sent up a silent prayer that God would help them work together, as well. Because if the chemical that had invaded Glen Lake was an act of terror, then they would have more to deal with than pride. Both countries would be at risk and lives at stake.

By the time Tessa reached the dock, her shoulder ached from the weight of her duffel bag. She hadn't realized how heavy the thing was. Regret for not allowing Jeff to take the bag when he'd offered intensified her tension. She didn't like needing help.

She'd decided long ago that relying on others for anything only led to disappointment, because no matter what she did or how hard she worked to please people, she never measured up. Therefore, if she didn't care what others thought and relied only on herself, her heart was safe. She was safe.

Resolute in that thought, she dropped the duffel holding her supplies on the wooden planks at her feet with a *thunk* and rolled her shoulders. She caught Jeff's gaze from the boat. Speculation lurked in the cobalt depths of his eyes.

She jerked her gaze away and stared into the water, focusing on what was at stake. The forest, the lake and the fish. Human lives.

"She's a beauty."

Jeff's words jerked Tessa's attention to the motorboat bobbing gently against the side of the dock. George stood inside the boat, showing Jeff around the helm.

She spied a Zodiac, an inflatable boat with an aluminum floor, lying upside down on the shore. Two black oars stuck straight up out of the sand beside it. She pointed. "That's what we're taking."

Jeff followed the trajectory of her finger. "You've got to be kidding me."

"Don't think you can handle it?" She picked up her bag. Maybe he'd relent and not insist on going with her. She preferred work-ing alone.

His lips thinned. "I can handle it." He climbed out of the motorboat and stalked down the dock.

She turned to George. "Do you have an-other set of oars?"

Amusement twinkled in his brown eyes. "Yes, ma'am." George handed her a map of the lake. Then he unclipped a walkie-talkie from his belt and held it out. "There's no cell service on the north end. Use this if you run into any trouble."

"Thanks." She slipped the walkie-talkie into the outside pocket of her bag.

Once they had the inflatable boat flipped and half in, half out of the water, Tessa tossed her duffel inside. It landed with a dull thud.

"What's in that bag?" Jeff asked as he climbed inside the boat and settled on the back transom.

"My testing kit and ten essentials. Every-thing needed to survive for a short time in the wilderness."

"We won't be getting out of the boat," Jeff muttered as he took an oar in each hand.

"You never know what you'll need." She threw one leg over the side, then the other, careful to keep the boat balanced by planting her feet wide. Then she sat on the middle bench seat facing Jeff. Tucking the second set of oars George handed her beneath the bench along with her bag, she shrugged. "I like to be ready for anything. You never know when disaster will strike."

One side of Jeff's mouth lifted. "You sound like an ad for FEMA."

She arched an eyebrow. "I attended the Center for Domestic Preparedness training."

His mouth quirked. "Me, too. Though it must have been at a different time. I'd have remembered you."

She rolled her eyes, not believing she would have garnered his attention at all then or now if it wasn't for this situation.

He cocked his head. "Hmm, maybe I should grab a few things."

The teasing tone in his voice grated on her nerves. "You should. I'll wait."

He blinked. "That's okay. We'll be back here by dinnertime. I ate a big lunch."

She shrugged. So had she. George had

brought her a sandwich piled high with ham and cheese, a side of fruit and a soda. But she liked to snack throughout the day. "Suit yourself."

She pulled on a pair of silicone gloves and grabbed two test tubes and a plastic baggie from her bag, then leaned over the side of the boat to fill two tubes with water. The boat height was perfect. She then removed two foil packets from the baggie, popped out two tabs, broke them into fourths and dropped a piece into each tube. She shook the water to dissolve the tablet pieces.

The water in one tube turned blue, indicating bacteria, not uncommon, and the other turned red, indicating a chemical component.

Keeping her expression neutral to not alarm either of the men, she used a permanent marker and wrote *the ranger station dock* on the label along the side of each tube before slipping the tubes into another plastic bag.

Jeff slid on a pair of sunglasses, then picked up the oars. "Ready?"

"Just a sec." Tessa withdrew sunglasses and a hat from her bag and shoved them both on. "Now I am."

George pushed the boat off the sand. Soon they were floating. Jeff used the oars to turn the boat so they headed away from the dock. His well-defined biceps drew her attention. The guy obviously worked out. She appreciated when a man took care of himself.

She forced herself to look away. That he was fit aided in what they were doing. That was the only reason she'd even noted his athleticism.

They rowed from location to location along the lake's surface while she collected and tested samples. The dead fish floating around the boat saddened her.

"Can you row that way?" She pointed to a sandy stretch of the shore. "There's something weird with the sand over there."

Jeff dug the oars into the water, propelling the boat in the direction she'd indicated. When the Zodiac slid firmly onto the sandy shore, Tessa scrambled out of the boat to inspect what at first appeared to be a dark stain in the sand.

But on closer inspection, the dark line was some kind of moisture slowly flowing into the lake from the trees. The putrid stench of decay coming from the liquid assaulted her senses.

Heart racing, she ran back to the boat to grab her testing supplies. Jeff walked toward the trees while she returned to the mystery fluid and tested it.

As the results presented themselves, her stomach twisted in dread and triumph.

With a blue and a red vial in hand, she called to Jeff, "This is the source of the contamination."

With Tessa's words echoing in his head, Jeff stopped at the tree line and stared into the thick ancient forest, where the nasty runoff seemed to originate.

This area was unpopulated and rugged with dense underbrush, towering evergreens, maples and alders, making the woods dark and forbidding.

What was causing the lethal runoff? Had someone been using the forest for chemical waste? Was the noxious substance caused by an accident, or had someone purposely released it? To what end?

The questions spun in his head, making his temples pound.

His first inclination was to charge into the woods to find the cause and put a stop to the polluted flow. They were on American soil. His jurisdiction. His hand rested on the butt of his holstered gun. But he couldn't do that part of his job, not while he was responsible for Tessa.

He spun around to look at the woman heading back to the boat. She may know her business around fish, but her domain was the lab, not the wilderness. Despite her bag of essentials, she wouldn't last more than a few hours in this terrain.

He blew out a breath. He couldn't leave her here by herself. Besides, there was no way she'd agree to being left behind, anyway.

The best course of action was to report what they'd found and let the sheriff and the professionals who knew how to deal with toxic waste handle this situation. He slipped his cell phone out of his pocket. No signal. *Great.*

The roar of an outboard motor revved through the air. A speedboat, carrying two men dressed in camouflage, zipped along the water's surface heading in their direction.

Jeff clenched his jaw. Probably hunters. Ranger Harris and Sheriff Larkin had shut down the lake. These two jokers were going to be in big trouble. He'd report the boat's bow number to the sheriff when he returned to the ranger station.

Shaking his head with frustration, Jeff stalked back toward Tessa. She sat in the boat fiddling with a walkie-talkie. Resourceful woman.

She glanced up and yelled, "I can't get this thing to work!"

The engine on the speedboat cut to an idle and diverted Jeff's attention away from Tessa. Both men pulled bandannas over the lower half of their faces, and one of the men hefted a rifle to his shoulder, aiming the weapon at Tessa.

Horror flooded Jeff's system. He grabbed his sidearm. "Tessa! Get down!"

# TWO

A startling bang followed by an even louder pop jolted through Tessa. One side of the Zodiac deflated like a balloon pricked by a needle. She was being shot at!

She dived to the floor of the boat. More gunfire erupted. The shocking sound vibrated through her, making her heart pound so hard she thought it would explode out of her chest.

Jeff jumped over the still-inflated side of the Zodiac, landing with a thump beside her. He log-rolled onto his back, his gun in front of him, aimed toward the lake. "You okay?"

"Yes. You?"

He fired off two rounds. The deafening noise reverberated inside her head. She reached beneath the bench seat for the Zodiac's emergency kit, grabbed the flare gun and clutched it to her chest.

"Please, God…help." The whispered prayer slipped out, dredged up from a suppressed place deep within her soul.

She flipped onto her back and aimed toward the boat, preparing to fire.

Jeff shook his head. "No. We may need that."

The speedboat roared away. They were leaving. Relief made her melt into the floor.

Jeff jumped to his feet and tugged on her arm. "They're circling back. Get up. We have to run for the trees."

Galvanized by fear and adrenaline, she scrambled out of the boat. Her ears rang, and her temples throbbed. Jeff grabbed her duffel bag and tugged her along.

"Wait! The walkie-talkie!" She'd dropped it on the bottom of the boat. It was the only way of reaching help. She turned to run back.

The speedboat raced toward the shore.

Bullets slammed into the ground, spitting up pieces of sand that bit her flesh through her pant leg. She let out a yelp as she skidded in the loose soil, her arms windmilling as she fought to keep her balance. Her mind screamed, *Run for your life!* while her practical side yelled, *Get the walkie-talkie!* It could be the only way they survived.

"Leave it!" Jeff's shouted command overrode her inner conflict. He captured her by the waist, hauling her off her feet, and ran with her in one arm and her duffel gripped in the other hand.

More bullets whizzed past, hitting the earth, the trees. Tessa gripped Jeff's arm with a fresh wave of panic. What if he was hit trying to protect her? She hated the thought of someone being hurt on her account.

Once they reached the shelter of the forest, he set her on her feet. "Go!" he urged, giving her a slight push.

She ran, charging through the underbrush, not caring that branches snagged at her clothes and twigs snapped beneath her heels. They were running for their lives. But at least they were alive to run.

Finally, Jeff tugged her behind the huge trunk of a Douglas fir. Dropping the bag on the ground, he pressed close to her, his six-foot frame crowding her personal bubble.

Normally, she didn't like when anyone invaded her space, but she found comfort in the protection he so easily and willingly extended. That it was part of his job didn't matter. She'd take it.

Her breathing came in ragged gasps. She willed her heart rate to slow. Blinking up at him, she asked, "What do we do now?"

He leaned sideways to peer around the tree toward the lake, then straightened to meet her gaze. "Pray. And thank God for the forest."

Was he being glib?

Looking into the depths of his blue eyes, she saw sincerity. "Praying's good."

Holding her gaze, he said, "Lord, we ask for Your protection. We ask that You would guide us out of these woods safely. In Your Son's name, amen."

Quick and painless. But would the words be effective? She'd had so many unanswered prayers in her life, she wasn't sure God really listened. At least not to her. "Amen."

Jeff stepped back and surveyed their surroundings. "We can't go back the way we came. Obviously, someone isn't happy we're investigating the contamination."

Tessa dropped to her knees and dug through her bag. "Ranger Harris gave me a map of the area." She tugged the folded map out of the pocket she'd stuffed it in.

Jeff knelt down beside her to help unfold the map. He pointed to a spot along the lakeshore. "This is where our boat is." He moved his finger in a straight line through the forest section and stopped. "We're probably about here."

They'd gone approximately three hundred feet. She studied the map. "Look. There's a fire road here."

"That's about twenty miles west."

She glanced to her right to where the nasty substance marred the forest floor. "The same direction the toxin's flowing from."

He nodded. "We'll either come across the source of the pollutant first or the fire road."

She had an awful suspicion that finding the source would be detrimental to their well-being. "And when we get to the road, then what?"

"We follow it back to civilization."

"And help." She was glad she'd worn her older, broken-in boots, though she hadn't counted on a trek in the woods. Remembering she had a compass in her duffel, she dug the small device out to verify the direction they needed to travel.

He stood, his body tense as he looked from her to their surroundings. "We have to pay attention to signs of life, human and animal. We don't want to go tramping into a cougar habitat or come upon a pack of gray wolves unawares."

"This isn't my first foray into the woods, you know." She'd been trained in wilderness survival techniques. Not that she'd ever had to use them.

He cocked an eyebrow. "I'm sure those situations weren't like this."

She folded the map and stowed it away in the pocket of her duffel. "No, they weren't. Most of the fieldwork I do is with teams responsible for the protection and restoration of fish habitat management. I rarely venture far from the water's edge. And I've never been shot at." She quaked, recalling how close those bullets had come. After tucking the flare gun inside the bag, she zipped it up and stood.

"Here, let me take that." He reached for her bag.

She hesitated. Part of her wanted to let him carry her load. But that wouldn't be fair. She'd brought the duffel; she should be responsible to carry her bag. "I've got it."

His expression hardened. "We need to move quickly. It's only going to slow you down."

Accepting his rationale was easier than accepting his help. She relinquished her hold on the duffel. "You're right. Thank you."

He settled the strap across his body. "Why didn't you bring a team with you to the lake?"

She shrugged, trying to downplay the truth. "I felt a strong urging that I needed to get to Glen Lake quickly."

For expedience's sake, she'd advocated traveling to Glen Lake alone to assess the damage and then decide if a full team would be required to make the trek to Washington State. She'd hoped the fish kill was something simple, something that could be easily contained.

Unfortunately, that clearly wasn't the case. Once they returned to the ranger station, she'd report in. By then the team would have been assembled and ready to move.

"You listened to your gut feeling." He sounded approving. "In my line of work, that could make the difference between life and death."

If what happened earlier was any indication of the type of situations he alluded to, she was glad she worked with fish, not criminals. She admired and respected men and women who put their lives at risk for others. It took courage and commitment. And apparently faith.

"Has it?" she asked. "I mean, has your gut feeling saved your life?"

He held her gaze. "Yes. Though I prefer to think that God was prompting me rather than it having anything to do with me."

"Interesting." She wasn't sure what she thought about his statement. Had God ever prompted her? Until today it had be a long time since she'd thought about faith. She couldn't honestly say where she stood with God.

Needing to put them back on track, she said, "We should go."

After a heartbeat, he looked away, releasing his hold on her. She filled her lungs with deep breaths as if she'd been deprived of oxygen. Shaking off his effect, she put one foot in front of the other and moved forward.

Jeff gestured to the trees. "See the patterns of the woods? The areas of light that seep through the canopy of tree branches? The dark places are where an animal would be most likely to hide. If we pay attention, the forest can tell us a lot about the creatures that live here."

Apparently, he'd had some wilderness training, too. She glanced around. Though she still saw the ecological environment that could be broken down into fascinating individual pieces, she also saw the complex system of living organisms and an ecosystem that held dangers as well as secrets. "So in addition to running for our lives and keeping an eye out for more bad guys, what should we be looking for?"

"The obvious is footprints. The ground closer to the runoff will be softer and will show more, but we can't rely on just the obvious."

A cold knot formed in Tessa's stomach. "If an animal drank from this liquid…"

"We might come across a sick or dead animal."

She shuddered at the images that rose in her mind. A sick animal could be more dangerous than a frightened one. The beast wouldn't have the good sense to avoid them. Most wild animals preferred to steer clear of humans unless provoked. An injured or sick creature might feel threatened and attack. Danger lurked in every direction. She moved closer to Jeff. "What other signs?"

"Feeding signs, like clipped vegetation or buried carcasses. Sleeping places. Some animals, like the fox, sleep curled beneath a bush, which would flatten the ground cover."

They moved deeper into the forest. Keeping her gaze alert, Tessa had to double her steps to keep up with his longer stride.

He brushed back the branches of a bush for her to pass through a thicket. "Rub spots, hair or feathers. Scat. Travel routes, places where the vegetation is packed down and bruised, or spots where the leaves have been disturbed or berries of a bush have been stripped or twigs broken or grass bent."

On the plane over from Utah, she'd read up on the national park. There'd been numerous sightings of cougars this past spring. As well as black bears and wolves. One report sighted a grizzly bear roaming the forest.

These woods covered thousands and thousands of acres across two countries. The likelihood that they'd run into a wild beast was slim. But not impossible.

Tension tightened the muscles between her shoulders. "How do you know so much about this stuff?"

"Through the U.S. Search and Rescue Task Force training."

"Is that normal for a border agent?"

He shrugged. "Not mandatory. But essential when covering acres of forestland. My job requires I know how to track humans through the woods."

She'd heard stories of people trying to enter the country illegally through the forests that separated the U.S. from Canada. Jeff's obvious commitment to his job, to his country, was admirable.

He held out a hand, stopping her. Pointing to the ground, he said, "See this?"

She stooped down to look closer and could make out a faint impression. "What is it?"

"Not sure. Could be the pad print of a mammal, like a fox, cat or raccoon. Or even a porcupine." His voice hardened. "Or the heel of a boot."

A shiver of apprehension shimmied down her back. She bent to inspect the liquid and the surrounding earth. "Either this fluid has been flowing for a long time or someone has made a shallow trench."

She hated that someone had deliberately funneled toxins into the lake. She couldn't imagine for what purpose other than to poison the water. Someone who would have such little regard for the environment and human life wouldn't think twice about killing them. A ribbon of fear snaked through her, raising the fine hairs at her nape.

In a low crouch, Jeff searched the ground in a wide radius. "That's the only impression I see."

"Is that good or bad?"

Shrugging, he straightened. "Both. Other than right next to the moist dirt, the ground is dry and solid. The dead leaves and fallen branches create a barrier, so the soil isn't exposed enough for more prints. But that doesn't mean we can't tell if an animal or a person passed through the forest duff."

He pointed out a broken twig. "Something came this way."

Tessa's anxiety kicked up, making her tightly strung nerves even more taut. The forest grew thicker, more oppressive the farther they ventured in. She pointed to their left, where the leaves of the forest floor had been disturbed. "And went that way."

They pressed on. Jeff halted abruptly, putting a hand out to gently touch her arm.

Apprehension crawled up her neck. Her mouth went dry. "What?"

He glanced around, behind them to the sides. "I don't know. I thought I heard something."

They stood still and silent for a long moment, letting the sounds of the forest settle. Tessa clenched her hands tight to keep from reaching for Jeff.

A bird chirped high in a tree off to the right.

A chipmunk scurried out of the bushes and darted past them.

Some of the tension visibly drained from Jeff. Tessa reached for her water bottle and drank a few sips to relieve the dryness in her throat. But the lukewarm water did nothing to ease the strain wreaking havoc on her system. They pressed on. Fatigue pulled at the muscles in her legs, making the journey more labored.

Jeff broke the silence. "Where'd you grow up?"

She slanted him a quick look. "Chicago. You?"

"Seattle. Do you have a boyfriend?"

Her steps faltered. "That's a little personal, don't you think?"

"Is it? Seems like a reasonable question to ask someone you're running for your life with."

"Does it matter?"

"Not to me," he said. "Just a question."

For some reason his answer annoyed her. "Why wouldn't you ask if I was married?"

He reached out to help her over a branch that lay across their path. "You don't wear a ring."

Placing her hand in his, Tessa stared, fascinated with the way his bigger, stronger hand engulfed her smaller one and by the contrast in their skin tone. Her white skin, dotted with freckles, was a trait handed down by her Irish heritage.

His suntanned, olive skin was earned protecting the border, but she wondered what he did on his days off. What were his hobbies, his passions? Did he have a family? She gave herself a mental shake. What was she doing? His personal life was none of her business. She yanked her gaze to his face and stepped over the branch. "Neither do you."

Releasing his hold on her, he moved away. "Which means I'm not married."

She hurried to stay in step with him. "Some guys don't wear rings."

"Neither do some women. But I would if I was. But I'm not." He arched an eyebrow. "So?"

She clenched her hand around her water bottle. "Not that it's any of your business, but no, I don't have a boyfriend. Do you have a girlfriend?"

"No time for one. What's your excuse?"

She let out a wry laugh. "The same, I suppose." Seemed they both had reasons for not being in a relationship, reasons that, apparently, neither cared to share.

"What do your parents do?"

She frowned. She didn't like discussing her family. Jeff glanced at her, clearly waiting for her answer. When she didn't respond, he stopped and glanced around. "This would be a good time for a break."

He led the way to a fallen maple and sat. He accepted the snack bar she offered and continued to stare at her as he ate. She wondered if he used the silent stare as an interrogation tactic.

She sighed and sat on the ground with her back against a tree. "Dad's a lawyer. Mom owns a floral-design shop. Yours?"

"Doctors."

The clipped way he answered sounded almost derisive. Interesting. Two could indulge in a little interrogation. She knew how to cross-examine. She'd certainly been on the receiving end of her father's inquiries enough. She leaned forward and placed her elbows on her knees. "What type?"

He crossed his arms over his chest. "Dad's a cardiologist and a professor at the University of Washington's medical school. Mom's a neurosurgeon."

"Impressive. Those are specialized practices. How come you didn't go into medicine?"

He scoffed, "Not my forte. Why did you become a fish biologist?"

That was an easy question. One she was often asked. "I grew up in the city but longed to be outdoors. I knew early I wanted to work for the Forest Service. After receiving my B.S. in environmental studies, I went on to get my master's in water science, then my Ph.D. in ecology."

"Your parents must be proud of you," he said.

She shrugged, wincing inwardly at the shaft of hurt tearing through her. "I suppose."

She was loath to admit she didn't have much of a relationship with either one of her parents so had no idea if they were proud or not. Neither had ever said the words to her.

He leaned forward, studying her as if she were a bacterium in a petri dish. "You don't know?"

"Mom thinks I should get married and have babies. Dad's glad I have a job." That was about as close to an affirmation from him as she'd get. Dad was a perfectionist who expected everyone else to live up to the same standards that he had set for himself regardless how impossible. Few people could keep up verbally with her father. A great trait in a lawyer, but not so much in a father or, apparently, a husband.

"That's pretty typical, isn't it?"

She tucked in her chin. "Why? Because I'm female? Aren't you getting pressure from your mom to settle down and give her grandchildren?"

He gave a resigned shake of his head. "No. My mom didn't have time for her own kid. She certainly wouldn't have time for grandchildren. I doubt she's given it any thought."

"What do you mean, she didn't have time for you?" What kind of father would Jeff be? Involved and committed or one who showed up late or not at all, like her dad?

"Doctors, remember?" He rose and placed the strap of her duffel across his body. "Their patients came first. Always."

Though his tone was even, she detected a hint of pain underlying his words. Her heart cramped with empathy. She scrambled to her feet. "Are your parents still together?"

"Yep. Nearly forty years. They still live in the same house."

"Wow, good for them."

He gave her a quick glance, then set off again.

She caught up to him. "Not many married couples stay together that long anymore. Marriage commitment doesn't seem to matter."

He appeared to be rolling her words around in his mind. "Yeah. I guess you're right. I've never thought about it that way. What about yours?"

Sadness invaded her chest. "Dad lives in a high-rise in Chicago and Mom moved to the Florida coast years ago."

He glanced at her. "When did they divorce?"

"When I was five. Each has been married a couple times more since then." New family units built. A new set of stepparents, and sometimes stepsiblings, to reject her, making her feel so very alone and unacceptable.

"That's rough."

"Yeah, it was. But I made it to adulthood in one piece." But not without scars.

The terrain climbed. Tessa's lungs grew tight from the change in altitude and the labor of their hike. She consulted the compass. They were on track, though the woods grew denser and more overgrown. The tangled tree branches overhead kept the forest shrouded in shadows and made the air cooler as the afternoon turned to dusk. Autumn temperatures in the Cascades could dip into the teens after dark. She hoped they found their way out before then. She didn't relish the idea of spending the night in the forest.

"Hey, hold up a sec," Tessa said. "I need something from my bag."

She moved to stand in front of him and couldn't help noticing the stubble on his firm, square jaw, or the width of his shoulders. They looked like they were made to carry heavy burdens. Her attraction to him was growing with every step they took. Why? She wasn't sure.

Maybe deep down in places she hated to examine, she was lonely.

But crushing after only a few hours with

him was absurd. She didn't want to be attracted to Agent Steele. She wanted to be professional, to earn his respect. But being shot at and forced to hide in the woods weren't exactly circumstances that led to professionalism.

Frustrated with herself, she used more force than necessary to unzip the duffel and retrieve her lightweight hoodie. She yanked it over her head, thankful for the extra layer of warmth.

A rustling in the bushes off to the right drew her focus. The leaves of the shrubs danced. Something moved through the brush. Something bigger than a chipmunk. A lot bigger. A knot of dread tightened her chest. "Something's in there."

Jeff touched her arm and whispered, "Behind the trees."

He motioned to their left, where a grouping of alder grew together, their trunks nearly touching, their branches interwoven in an embrace. They hurried behind the shelter of the tree trunks.

Tessa held her breath. Her heart slammed against her ribs. Was it a cougar? Were they

being stalked? Or was the predator in the
bushes something even more dangerous than
an animal protecting its territory?

# THREE

A loud guttural noise emanated from the rustling bushes. Alarm zipped through Jeff and raised the hair on his arms. He tucked Tessa safely at his back as they took refuge behind a stand of alder trees. He searched for a weapon other than his sidearm. Shooting an animal would be his last resort.

The large brown head of a bear poked over the top of the bushes.

"It's a grizzly." Jeff's stomach sank like a rock in the lake. "What's he doing here?"

The creature stomped through the brush, snapping limbs and branches like toothpicks. Dark eyes stared in their direction. Jeff moved farther behind the tree, trying to keep as little of himself visible as possible.

The bear rose onto its back legs, making

the beast well over eight feet tall. He lifted his nose in the air.

"My bag," Tessa whispered. "I have a can of bear spray."

Of course she did. Part of her essentials. Bless her preparedness.

He slipped the strap of her duffel off and laid it on the ground at her feet.

She dug around in the bag and then handed him a long, slender canister. "Here."

The spray consisted of hot red pepper and could shoot up to twenty feet. An effective deterrent in the case of an attack. Jeff hoped it wouldn't come to that. He held the can nozzle out, his finger hovering over the button. He kept his gaze to the left of the bear so the animal was in his peripheral vision.

Making eye contact could be perceived as a challenge. He didn't want to give the creature any reason to charge.

Tessa clutched the back of his shirt. "Should we climb the tree?"

"Bears can climb, too," he said softly in a neutral tone. If the bear heard them talking, he didn't want the beast to sense any panic.

"Not grizzlies."

"I wouldn't want to risk my life on that myth," he said. "I saw a YouTube video of a young grizzly that climbed fifty feet up a fir tree."

Her hand tightened on his shirt, pulling the fabric taut against his chest, much like the band of anxiety squeezing his lungs. "Then what?"

"We wait and hope he goes away?" he quipped, not sure what their move should be. He rested his free hand on his holstered gun. Taking down a bear with his Heckler & Koch P2000 service weapon wasn't impossible, just improbable. Not the best scenario.

"Please, Lord, make the bear go away," Tessa prayed aloud.

"Amen to that," he said.

The bear dropped back to all fours, his nose going to the ground. No doubt sniffing their trail, looking for his next meal.

Tension balled in Jeff's gut. "Do you have any snack bars left?"

"A few of them," Tessa said. "What are you thinking?"

"A distraction."

"You shouldn't feed the bear. He could get sick from human food."

"Would you rather he got sick off this human food?" He bumped his fist against his chest. She shook her head vehemently, her eyes wide with fear. "Do you have a better idea?"

She grabbed four bars from her pack. "Here."

"Trade places with me." Jeff stepped back to allow Tessa to slip in front of him. "Hold the spray. If he moves any closer, use it."

She nodded, her red curls bobbing softly. She'd lost her hat somewhere along the way. The elastic band holding back her hair had slipped almost all the way off. Hugging the tree, she gripped the can with one hand.

Quietly, he slit open the top of the bars, then chucked them to the right behind the bear. The food crashed through the bushes. The bear swung around with a growl. He pawed the ground. Waited a moment, then cantered off in the direction of Tessa's snacks.

Jeff snatched up Tessa's bag, grabbed her hand and pulled her away from the tree. They hustled in the opposite direction of the grizzly, moving quickly yet trying hard not to make much noise.

Every broken twig, every crunch of dried leaves beneath their feet rang out like the discordant notes of a gong calling the grizzly to his dinner feast. They continued onward, keeping parallel to the toxic runoff, but staying where the trees and bushes provided some cover.

Twenty minutes later, Tessa tugged her hand free from Jeff's. "I don't think he followed us."

Jeff drew to a halt and listened. The noises of the forest whispered over him. A bird flapping its wings in the trees. The rustle of branches in the early-evening breeze. And an out-of-place humming sound.

"Do you hear that?" Jeff asked Tessa.

"The buzzing? What is it? Bees?"

"I don't think so." He strained to listen. "It's more electrical-sounding."

"Like a generator," Tessa stated. "Does the Customs and Border Patrol use generators for the equipment you have out here?"

"Some are powered by generators and some use solar energy."

"Then one of the video cameras could be close by." Excitement lit her eyes. "We could find it and signal for help."

"Brilliant idea."

She gazed at him with an eager, expectant look in her gold-flecked eyes. "So, where are they?"

He laughed. "Like I have every location memorized?"

She made a face and brushed her hair back. "One could hope."

Jeff flexed his fingers to keep from reaching over to wrap a corkscrew curl around his finger. He'd always found ringlets appealing.

He gave himself a mental slap on the back of the head. They were here to do a job, not to explore the attraction arcing between them. Oh, yeah, he'd noticed the appreciative flicker in her eyes when she'd been sizing him up when they met. And she'd blushed so prettily when he'd acknowledged what she was doing. He'd like to see her blush again.

His gaze dropped to her lush lips. He wondered what she'd do if he kissed her.

*Whoa! Back up.* That wasn't going to happen. They were in the middle of the woods, running from gunmen and a bear. This was no place to be thinking about kisses.

"Let's keep moving," he said as much to himself as to her. "Hopefully, we're far enough away from the grizzly to avoid drawing his attention back to us. But we need to make some noise to keep from startling any other predators that might be in the area."

"I can't hold a tune, so singing's out," Tessa said as she fell into step with him.

Liking her pluck, he chuckled. "Good to know. Talking will suffice. Did you grow up in Chicago?"

She flashed him a rueful look. "I did. A few blocks off the lake on the north side of town."

"I've never been to Chicago. Is it worth visiting?"

"It's a lovely city." She went on to tell him all the many reasons he should take a trip to the Windy City. He liked listening to her voice. The melodic tone was soothing. He detected a hint of an accent in the way she dropped her *th* sound in *the* and replaced it with a *d*. So *the lake* became *d'lake*. The accent became more pronounced the longer they traveled. A clear sign of her fatigue.

The forest deepened, the trees growing more dense, shutting out the setting sun. Time seemed suspended. Sweat broke out on Jeff's back despite the dropping temperature. The electrical humming sound remained a background noise like an annoying mosquito, underscoring the chirp of birds, the ticking of insects. The vibrating noise wasn't necessarily growing louder, but not quieter, either.

Whatever was making the humming wasn't a small generator attached to a video camera. He wouldn't stake his life or Tessa's on the belief that finding the source of the sound would bring them anything but trouble. Like the toxin, it was out of place, an intrusion that shouldn't be there in the forest. A possible danger. One that may or may not prove to be deadly.

"Shouldn't we have hit the fire road by now?" Tessa asked, the strain of the afternoon trembling in her voice. Or was that a shiver from the cold?

All around them the world turned from bright and vibrant colors to monochrome grays as the waning light of dusk slowly and surely disappeared.

"We have to have traveled twenty miles by now."

He hated to disappoint her but he'd guess more like six miles. He kept that to himself. He checked the time on his phone. They'd been in the woods for nearly seven hours. And unfortunately still no cell service.

She stumbled on an exposed root.

He clamped his hand around her elbow. "You okay?"

She took a deep breath and straightened. "I'm good."

The woman wouldn't admit to any weakness. He let go and admired her willingness to endure. So much for his assumption that she was too high maintenance for the outdoors.

They trudged on as the oppressive darkness closed in around them. A wolf howled. Uncomfortably close. The glacial air invading the forest seeped through his shirt.

Hiking at night wasn't wise, especially as the terrain climbed, making the going more arduous. They didn't have a trail to follow through the dense foliage. Despite keeping up the constant dialogue, they could easily startle a wary animal in the dark or stumble over a fallen branch. "We need to stop and make camp until daylight."

"Shouldn't we keep going? The fire road can't be that far. I have a flashlight and head-lamp."

Of course she did. "Not a good idea. It's getting colder, a wind has picked up and even with light it's dangerous out here at night."

"Won't stopping make us sitting ducks?" she asked, her voice rising slightly. "The bad guys aren't going to stop, are they?"

"If they're smart, they are. Though if they'd wanted us dead, they'd have killed us by now. They want us in these woods."

"Maybe to give them time to clean up the toxic waste."

"That could be it." Or they were to be made into human targets. In which case, any light would be their enemy. "But injuring ourselves stumbling around in the dark isn't the only thing we have to worry about. It's what hunts in the dark. And if we're moving, we're prey."

"And stopping, we're not?"

"Hunkered down, we have a better shot of not being caught unawares."

There was the briefest of pauses before she said, "We'll need to build some sort of wind-break."

He shifted her duffel bag. "You wouldn't happen to have one in here, would you?" The thing weighed heavy across his shoulder.

"Unfortunately, no. But I do have a rain-coat."

That would help. "You were smart to bring this. I should have listened to you and packed a bag."

"I wish I'd packed more food. We gave the bear the last of my bars," she said, her voice quiet.

As if on cue his stomach grumbled. "I can skip a meal or two."

"Let's hope it's only the one."

To their left was the visible outline of a fallen tree stump. He ushered her over to the round chuck of wood and slipped the bag off his shoulder. "Can you check the stump roots to make sure they aren't wet? I'll gather some sticks."

He walked away in search of some sturdy,

full branches to use as a shield against the wind. When he had an armful gathered, he returned to the stump and laid them on the ground. "This should be enough."

Working side by side, they quickly created a windbreak from the chilling wind. Soon they had the evergreen tree boughs in place with the raincoat hanging over them, blocking the gusts of frigid air whistling through the trees.

"There," Tessa said, wiping her hands on her pants. "I haven't made one of these since college."

"Part of a class?"

"No, actually, the forestry club. We went nature camping at least twice a year."

She was full of surprises. "You have a seat," he said. "I'll stand watch."

"There's room for both of us to sit," she said. "You can keep watch from a seated position, can't you?"

The tone in her voice held an edge of challenge. And no doubt if he refused to sit, she'd refuse, too. He sat. She followed suit and tucked her bag between them.

Armrest or boundary?

She had nothing to worry about from him. He had no intention of crossing the boundary.

He may like the fish doctor and, sure, found her attractive and quick-witted and resourceful and generally good company, but a budding romance that had nowhere to go and would only end in heartache wasn't on his agenda.

Despite how self-reliant and independent Tessa was, she struck him as the type of woman who wanted a happily-ever-after. He didn't believe such a thing existed.

Despite his parents' long marriage, he couldn't say they were happy. But then he'd never asked them if they were.

Frowning as he turned the thought over in his head, he settled into a semicomfortable position with his back propped against the stump, his hand on the butt of his holstered weapon.

Not ready to commit to approaching his parents with the question of their happiness, he tucked all thoughts of his family away.

Getting to safety and putting a stop to the water pollutant were his priorities. Until he knew this situation wasn't going to turn into an international crisis, he had to bring on his A-game. That meant staying alert and ignoring his attraction to the woman beside him or thoughts of marriage or family or happily-ever-afters.

The sound of Tessa's jacket scraping along the tree roots as she moved to a more comfortable position brought his attention to the moment. She was a trouper, that was for sure. Not one complaint about being cold or tired or uncomfortable. His respect for her continued to grow.

She shifted again. Her head came to rest against his biceps.

His blood pressure spiked. He gritted his teeth. Not for the life of him would he shake her off.

She jerked upright. "Sorry."

"Don't be. You're welcome to use my shoulder as a pillow."

"No, we should stay awake."

"Don't worry. I'm sure Ranger Harris and the sheriff have a search party out looking for us. We'll make it back to civilization long before we starve or freeze to death."

"I'll hold you to that." There was a smile in her voice.

Though her face was shadowed, there was enough ambient light for him to see the fatigue around her eyes and in the tightness of her shoulders.

"Tell me about Seattle," she said, her voice low. "I hear it rains all the time."

He laughed. "That's just something we tell people so they don't move there."

"What? It's not true?"

"No," he admitted. "But neither is Seattle the wettest city in the U.S. The Southeast gets more rain than the Pacific Northwest."

"Really? That seems odd."

He explained about a study he'd recently read. They debated the finer points of living where it rained versus snowed like where she resided in Utah.

"We get some snow where I live in Blaine," he commented. "Though it makes a mess of the traffic going in and out of the country when it happens."

"I can imagine." She yawned. He let the silence envelop them. He hoped she'd rest. Slowly, his senses adjusted to the nocturnal sounds, keenly in tune to the world around them, on the alert for any threat, both the two-legged kind and the four-legged kind.

"Tessa." Jeff's voice forced her eyes open.

She shook off sleep to listen to the high-pitched whistles of marmots, several of them if the racket they were making was any indication. Underscoring the squirrellike creatures' calls was the drumming of a nearby grouse, a chickenlike bird that inhabited the subarctic regions of the northern hemisphere. The rapping of a woodpecker added to the cacophony.

The first fingers of dawn crept through the tree branches, stinging her retinas and stirring her guilt. She'd fallen asleep, left Jeff to keep watch. "I'm so sorry!"

"No worries," his deep voice rumbled.

Slowly, her gaze shifted to where he stood, tall and intimidating with his hand outstretched. His uniform was dirty and disheveled, but nothing could take away from his rugged good looks. Her eyes met his stunning blue ones. Eyes she could get lost in. Her heart picked up speed, setting off an alarm bell inside her head.

She'd spent too much of her life displaced at the whims of her parents, then her ex-fiancé, Michael. He'd wanted to meld and mold her into a different person. It had taken all her courage and strength to break his hold on her life before she committed herself to marriage.

Because unlike her parents, once she married, it would be forever.

Losing herself again wasn't going to happen. At least not now, not with this guy. They had a job to do. Nothing more. *Get a grip.*

"We need to get moving," he coaxed.

Wide-awake and eager to be gone from this forest, she scrambled to her feet without his offered help and inhaled the crisp morning air. Her stomach rumbled with hunger. Her limbs ached from yesterday's excursion. She rubbed the kink in her neck.

Jeff walked over to a lush, tall plant. Tessa blinked, her gaze sweeping over the multitude of similar plants growing among the trees in dense rows all around them. Surprise squeezed her lungs tight. "Uh, Jeff. Do you know what those plants are?"

He picked a leaf, bringing the broken foliage to his nose. "Yep." He lifted his gaze to meet hers. "I'd say we've walked into a major grow."

She swallowed as the implications of his words reverberated through her mind. They were looking at hundreds of thousands, if not millions, of dollars' worth of marijuana, and that was only the plants they could see. Who knew how far-reaching the expanse of the pot farm went?

"A grow like this would be watched and closely guarded." Anxiety twisted in her chest, making her heart rate double. "We need to make tracks and fast."

"Tessa, look." Jeff pointed to the overflowing pipes of an irrigation system. A current of fluid flooded from in between the pot plants and flowed along the forest floor. The conduit for the toxin. Gravity did the work of taking the contaminated liquid all the way to the lake. "Must be some sort of insecticide in the water."

"This is bad. Real bad."

In two long strides, he reached her side and cupped her elbow. "We need to head in the opposite direction and pray we make it to the road undetected."

"Too late for that," said a deep male voice from behind Tessa.

She whirled around. A dozen men dressed in camouflage with bandannas covering the lower half of their faces stepped out of the forest like chameleons. Each man held a nasty-looking rifle aimed at her and Jeff.

They were surrounded with no way out.

The man who had spoken—clearly their leader—raked his gaze over her before his flat, lizardlike eyes met hers. "It's a pleasure, Dr. Cleary."

Tessa gaped. How did the man know who she was?

Jeff tugged her behind him. "Who are you?"

"Your worst nightmare, Agent Steele."

"I doubt that," Jeff stated, his voice hard.

"We shall see." The man flicked his wrist at them.

From behind her, a bag came down over Tessa's head. She yelped with surprise.

"Hey!" Jeff shouted. She heard a sickening

thud. Had they hit him? Killed him? Panic clogged her throat and seized her lungs.

Rough hands ripped her away from Jeff's side and dragged her into the forest.

# FOUR

Tessa gasped for air inside the burlap sack that had been thrown over her head and pulled tight. She struggled against the restraints holding her hands behind her back, desperately wishing she could claw the bag away and take a deep, clean breath. She'd never take oxygen for granted again.

Despite her best efforts, panic constricted her throat; her lungs burned from breathing in her own carbon dioxide. She resisted the man's rough hand clamped around her upper arm like a manacle, but he was too strong. He forced her to stumble forward at a fast clip.

Were they marching her to her death? The panic increased. She hyperventilated. Dots appeared before her eyes. No. She wouldn't pass out. She fought to stay conscious.

Where was Jeff? After his shout, he'd gone silent. Did that mean they'd separated them? Had they killed him?

Her chest caved in at the thought. "Jeff!" she screamed.

"Here" came his muffled reply.

A measure of relief loosened the tightness cramping her insides. This was her fault. If she'd waited for the full team to assemble... they all might be prisoners now, not just her. And Jeff.

"Put her in the back." The harsh command came from the leader, the one who'd looked at her like a choice steak he wanted to devour. She shivered with distaste.

Hands hauled her off her feet. She kicked wildly, connecting with hard muscles and bone. Her captor let out a satisfying yelp of pain. She was dumped sideways on a hard metallic surface.

She heard Jeff's groan as he landed next to her. She scooted toward him, until her arm bumped his broad back. His arms were twisted behind him. His bound hands gripped the fabric of her jacket.

"We'll be okay," he told her, his voice barely audible.

"No talking!" a voice ordered.

A thud jolted through her—an impact of something hard hitting something soft. Jeff grunted in pain. Tessa could only imagine what assault he'd suffered for trying to reassure her. Though she appreciated his effort, she wasn't naive enough to believe they would get out of these woods alive. It made her sick. Doors slammed. The roar of an engine rumbled beneath them. They were inside a vehicle. From the pinging of rocks on the underbelly and the echoing noise of the bumpy terrain, she guessed a cargo van of some sort. They were being driven away from the pot field, away from the toxic runoff. Away from any chance at surviving.

No! She wouldn't think that way. There must be something they could do, some way for them to escape. They hadn't killed them outright. That was good, wasn't it?

*Please, dear God in Heaven, we need You. Please, please protect us.*

She hoped God was listening. Even as the thought formed, she chastised herself for being one of those people who only looked to God in their time of need. Her grandma Vida would be so disappointed.

The one bright spot in Tessa's life had been her grandmother on her mom's side. Grandma Vida had had a deep faith in God and had hoped to instill that faith in Tessa. But hearing about God when Grandma visited once or twice a year hadn't been enough to convince Tessa to rely on Him.

But facing a forest full of men with guns apparently revived what little faith Tessa had absorbed.

By the time the vehicle came to a jerking halt, Tessa's body felt bruised and sore. Doors opened. Hands grabbed her by the feet and dragged her along the floor of the van before tipping her upright so her feet were on solid ground. The sunlight filtering in through the burlap material assaulted her eyes. The humming noise was louder here.

"Take them to the holding cell."

She didn't like the idea of that, but at least she and Jeff would be together. She wanted to believe that together they would find a way out of this.

An unseen man led her forward. Gravel

crunched beneath their feet. She heard the squeak of a door hinge. The bag was removed from her head. She blinked as her eyes adjusted to the light. She was standing in front of the open door of a wooden toolshed.

"Go in." The man at her side was young, maybe twenty, with long, stringy hair and dull brown eyes. He didn't look like a killer.

"Please, help us," Tessa pleaded in a low voice.

"Go in," the young man repeated more firmly this time before his now-fearful gaze darted past Tessa. "Hurry."

Following his gaze, Tessa saw a big, burly man with a ragged scar down one side of his face shove Jeff, who still wore a bag over his head, toward them. The burly man *did* look like a killer. Or at least what she imagined one to look like, but she'd never faced one before, so she really didn't know. Hysteria danced at the edges of her mind. A chill chased down her spine. She hung on to her self-control by a thread.

The younger man pushed Tessa. She stumbled into the shed.

"Get in there," the burly man barked as he thrust Jeff inside.

Jeff fell to the floor. The door slammed shut. For a moment, the young man peeked through the small window in the door before disappearing from view. A side window provided light but no air to the dank space.

"Tessa?" Jeff got to his knees.

"Here." She went to him. "Stay down for a sec. Let me try to get the hood undone." She turned her back to him. Her bound hand fumbled with the hood but she managed to work it up and off his head.

When she turned around to look at him, she gasped. Blood trickled from the corner of his mouth. A bruise formed on his cheek. "You're hurt."

"Not bad." He got his feet beneath him and walked to the window. "We're in some sort of compound."

She joined him and peered out. Two buildings were visible. Several young men walked by.

"We need to get untied," Jeff said. "Turn around and let me get those ropes off you."

She felt his hands tugging at the knot holding her wrists together. She winced as the rough material cut into her flesh. Then the bonds loosened enough that she could wiggle her hands free. "You did it."

She hurried to untie the rope wound around his wrists. The knot was stubborn, but she prevailed. The rope dropped away.

"Good job." Jeff moved to inspect the door, the walls.

Rubbing her wrists, she said, "How long do you think they'll keep us here?"

"No telling. I'm not sure why they are keeping us alive."

"We're going to die, aren't we?" She hated the panic rising in her voice.

He moved to her side and cupped her cheek. "We'll find a way out of here. God expects me to do all I can and trust the rest to Him."

His words were reassuring. But the dread in her middle didn't lessen one bit. She searched his eyes and saw the same certainty reflected back at her—they were trapped in a four-by-six shed with no way out. Escape was their only option. But how?

Jeff kept watch out the window. One of the two visible buildings appeared to be the mess hall. Several young men came out carrying plates of food. His mouth watered, and his stomach cramped.

He inspected the hinges of the door for the umpteenth time. There was no way to pry the hinges apart from the inside without some sort of knife. His had been taken when they confiscated his utility belt along with his service weapon. He should have hidden the blade in his boot before they set out. He shoved his hand through his hair. He should have been more prepared for something like this happening.

"You should save your energy." Tessa sat against the sidewall, her knees drawn to her chest.

He paced. "I'm too keyed up to sit."

The sound of the lock on the door unlatching sent Jeff's heart racing. Tessa jumped to her feet, her eyes wide with anxiety. He hurried to a position by the door so he could ambush whoever came in.

The door opened. A young guy walked in carrying a tray of food. He paused, noting their untied hands. He shrugged. "I'd have to untie you so you could eat, anyhow."

Jeff hesitated. No way would they let this unarmed kid come alone.

"Set the tray down and come out," a harsh male voice called.

Jeff peered around the corner of the door. A behemoth of a man stood two feet away with a rifle pointed at the teen's back. He was too far away for Jeff to disarm him, and if he tackled the kid and used him as leverage, the guy with the rifle wouldn't think twice about shooting them both.

The kid set the tray down laden with two sandwiches of indeterminate meat and cheese and two bottles of water.

Tessa moved close to the young man and whispered, "Please, you have to help us."

The guy straightened and backed out, showing no sign of hearing her plea.

Then the door slammed shut.

Jeff smashed a fist into the wall. Pain reverberated up his arm.

"At least they're feeding us. That has to be a good sign, right?" Tessa asked as she picked up a sandwich.

"Wait." He held up a hand. "We don't know that they haven't laced this food with poison."

She made a questioning face. "Why go to the bother of poisoning us? That's a murder weapon with no control when they could simply shoot us."

"Poison would be a lot harder to trace than a bullet slug."

Tessa stared at the sandwich in her hand. "Unfortunately, that makes sense." Her gaze rose to his. "How strong is your faith?"

"What?"

"You pray, so you obviously believe in God. Do you trust Him to keep us alive? To get us out of these circumstances?" There was a note in her tone that was almost pleading, as if she needed his faith to be strong.

His faith had never been tested like this before. He'd faced gunmen, had had his heart ripped from his chest by a woman and had felt abandoned by his family for most of his childhood, but he'd found comfort in his faith. He'd resented the many camps his parents had sent him to until his thirteenth summer, when he'd given his life to Jesus. That summer had been life changing.

And now Tessa was asking him to prove the strength of his faith.

"I do trust Him. God will not abandon us. God would expect me to be smart and take action. To know not to trust them." He gestured toward the door and the miscreants beyond.

She set the sandwich down and moved back to her spot against the wall. "Then we won't eat."

Her belief in him touched him deeply. He picked up the bottles of water and inspected them. The seals hadn't been broken. He moved to her side, slid down to sit next to her and handed her a bottle. "People will be looking for us."

"I know. But will they find us?" The despair in her eyes tore at his heart. "We don't know how far from the lake they've taken us."

"I was paying attention, counting out the seconds on the drive here. We're not more than a ten-minute ride from where they found us in the woods."

"From what I could see of this place, it's been here a long time. Undetected."

"Because no one knew to look." He covered her hand with his. "You can't lose hope."

"I never pegged you for an optimist."

"And I never pegged you as a pessimist."

"Guilty as charged. I guess if you get knocked down enough, you start to expect it."

He ached at the hurt in her tone. "You were put through the wringer with your parents. But I sense there's more." He thought back to her question about why he didn't have a girlfriend. His answer had been less than the truth. Her answer had mirrored his. "What's the guy's name who hurt you?"

She met his gaze, then looked away. "Michael. Michael Compton. I almost became Mrs. Compton."

"Ah. He cheated on you." Typical story.

Shaking her head, she said, "No. That actually might have been easier to deal with."

"Meaning?"

She stood and paced. "Meaning, Michael had his idea of what a wife should be. And as much as I thought I loved him, I couldn't fit into his mold. Everything I did was wrong. My choice of career, my wardrobe. Even the car I drove wasn't good enough."

"Sounds like a jerk. How long were you with this guy?"

"Four years. We met the first week of my

doctoral program at Utah State University and were engaged the following year. I was already working for the Forest Service part-time. He thought it was something I would do until after we were married and started a family."

"I get that. He feared you wouldn't make your family the priority."

"Exactly. And he wouldn't listen when I said I could do both. Women work and raise families all the time."

"Or hire others to raise their families." The bitterness rising burned his tongue.

"Nannies?" She retook her seat beside him.

"A string of them." He let out a rueful laugh. "I was a handful."

One side of her mouth lifted. "I'm envisioning you putting creepy, crawling things in your nannies' pockets."

"I'll admit to a few garter snakes popping up in strategic places."

They shared a smile. He admired how brave she was being considering they were locked up, hungry, tired and terrorized.

When her smile faded and her gaze drifted

to the food a few feet away, he said, "So what happened? Did he call off the wedding?"

"No. He expected us to move to his hometown in Upstate New York, which I didn't have a problem with. I applied for a position in the Rome Fish Disease Control Lab. It would have been an easy commute. But that wasn't going to fly. So I called off the wedding."

Her career had been more important than the relationship. At least she'd been honest about it, unlike Janie had been with him. She'd said all the right things, but in the end, when she'd been offered a promotion that took her to Asia, she'd left him in the dust. "You did the right thing."

"It was one of the hardest things I've ever had to do."

"But better to do it before making a commitment you couldn't keep."

She drew back. "You're starting to sound like Michael."

He shrugged. "If you can't give a hundred percent to your marriage, your family, then you shouldn't get married. And that's true for a man or a woman."

She blew out a breath. "So I take it that's why you aren't married? Because you can't commit?"

He lifted a shoulder. "Partly."

"Why else?"

He grew uncomfortable under her scrutiny, but answered honestly, "I don't believe in love."

She tucked in her chin. "But you believe in God."

"That's different."

"How?"

"Because God is God and the rest of us are, well, flawed and incapable of putting others before ourselves."

She canted her head, her gaze troubled. "That's pretty jaded."

Maybe so, but better jaded than hurt. Hoping to steer the conversation away from himself, he asked, "How did Michael take your calling off the wedding?"

"He was crushed. Told me I had led him on, made him believe we'd be together forever." A frown appeared between her eyebrows. "He went so far as to say if he couldn't have me, he didn't want anyone else to. Kind of scared me."

Jeff's hands curled into fists. "I would think so. Did he...hurt you?"

"No, thankfully. He was all talk. We parted ways, but it taught me to be more careful."

"How long ago was this?"

"It's been three years."

"Have you dated since then?" he asked, more curious than he should be.

"A few first dates."

"No second dates?" He was sure there were plenty of men who'd want a second date with a woman like her.

She shrugged. "Like I said, I'm careful."

He couldn't fault her. Not when he didn't do second dates, either.

The sound of the lock sliding open galvanized them both to their feet.

The same young man who had brought the food shuffled in.

He looked at the uneaten food and then looked at them, his eyes big and scared. "They'll get mad if you don't eat."

"Who's *they?*" Jeff walked closer.

The kid backed up. "You better not try anything," he said in a low, urgent tone with a quick glance over his shoulder. "They'll kill you. And me."

"Where are we?" Tessa asked.

"Sherman's place." The kid stuffed his hands into his pockets. "You better eat that quick."

"Get out here!" a man from beyond the open door to the shed shouted.

Jeff stepped to the right so he had a line of sight on the big guy with the scar running down the side of his face. The AK-47 the man held was aimed at the door.

"Did they put something in the food?" Tessa asked.

The kid scrunched up his nose. "No. I brought it straight over from the kitchen."

"Then we better hurry." Jeff touched Tessa's shoulder. "Grab them off the tray."

Once she had the sandwiches stacked in her hands, Jeff swept the tray off the floor and handed it to the younger man. "I'm Jeff. This is Tessa. What's your name?"

After a moment of hesitation, he answered, "Kyle."

Releasing his hold on the tray, Jeff nodded. Kyle hurried out the door, locking it behind him.

"Here." Tessa pressed a sandwich into his hand.

The thing was dry and tasted like cardboard, but he ate every last crumb.

Tessa took a swig of water. "I wonder who Sherman is."

"I have a suspicion we'll find out soon enough." Jeff reached for his own water bottle and drank deeply.

"Why did you ask Kyle his name?" Tessa asked. "And tell him ours?"

"If we hope to sway him to our side, he has to see us as people, as friends."

"Smart. I'm impressed."

"I don't know if it will work. Kyle's afraid of the man with the scar."

"Do you blame him?" She scrunched up her nose and frowned. "That guy creeps me out."

"Me, too." He finished off his bottle of water.

"Shouldn't you save some?" Tessa asked, concern darkening her eyes.

Taking the empty bottle, he blew into it,

then quickly tightened the cap. Grasping each end of the bottle in his hands, he twisted the plastic cylinder until there were two bubbled sections.

"What are you doing?"

"Making a water-bottle gun. When I release the pressure by twisting the cap, the cap will pop off with force. It won't kill anyone but hopefully it will distract enough for me to disarm whoever comes through that door again."

"But that guy with the scar stands too far back."

He winced. "Yeah. That's a problem."

"How did you learn that trick?"

"Science class in junior high." He grinned. "I never thought it would come in handy but…" He shrugged. "Here's hoping it works when the time comes."

He went to the window and peered out. He could tell from the position of the sun that it was well past noon. He prayed his boss had sent out a search party when Jeff didn't check in.

He counted the men he saw coming and going from the two buildings he could see.

Only a couple of the guys were armed. He wished he'd caught a better look at the place to determine how heavily defended they were. He knew there were at least a dozen men with guns. But was that it or were there more? He needed to know how far away the nearest town was and where the road they were brought in on led.

He heard voices before he saw two men appear in his line of sight from the side of the hut. He backed away from the window so they wouldn't see him.

The rattle of the lock sent his pulse skyrocketing.

He held his makeshift weapon at the ready and prayed for an opportunity to escape.

# FIVE

Jeff stood to the side of the doorway. His body was visibly coiled tight with tension as he held the bottle in front of him at the ready. Tessa sent up a silent plea to God that Jeff's plan didn't backfire and get him killed. The door swung open. Every muscle and nerve in her body snapped to attention.

Kyle stepped in. "The boss wants to see you two."

Jeff relaxed his stance. Tessa let out a tight breath.

Kyle's nervous gaze darted from Jeff's face to the water bottle and back again. "I wouldn't try anything," Kyle whispered. "He'll kill you."

"He'll kill us, anyway," Jeff shot back.

"Not without the boss's permission." He

made a face and added in a whisper, "Or unless you do something stupid."

"Get out here!" the guard snapped in a loud, angry tone.

"Leave it," she whispered to Jeff, pointing at the bottle. "Don't give him a reason to hurt you."

He hesitated, clearly debating the wisdom of taking the water-bottle gun with him. Finally, he set the makeshift weapon in a dark corner near the door.

She took Jeff's outstretched hand, grateful not to be alone in this nightmare.

They followed Kyle out of the shed. The guy with the nasty scar had his equally nasty-looking rifle pointed at their hearts.

Kyle led them away from the hut toward a small house fitted with a ramp instead of stairs leading to the front door.

Jeff nudged her in the side with his elbow. When she glanced his way, he gestured with his chin to her right. She turned her gaze to find herself looking at a large greenhouse surrounded by tall marijuana plants. There was a warehouse a little farther away. Also a large generator. The origin of the vibrating sound they'd heard. But what interested her most were the two jeeps and a van. Probably the same van they'd arrived in.

If they could get to one of them, they could escape. But that was a big *if.*

She noticed that several men, ranging in age from younger than Kyle to old and gray, stopped whatever they were doing to gawk at them. Why were there no women?

At the house, Kyle opened the door and stepped aside.

"You're not coming in?" Tessa asked the younger man.

He shook his head before scurrying away.

"Move it," the guard said as he prodded her forward with the tip of his weapon.

Jeff growled and stepped in front of her. "Don't touch her."

Tessa shivered at the menace in Jeff's expression as he confronted the other man. Though his scarred face appeared carved in stone, the thug gave way a step.

"Come in, please," a voice called from inside the open door.

Tessa turned to see a man in a wheelchair waving them inside. He had silver hair and a full white beard that concealed most of his ruddy complexion. Light gray eyes regarded her intently. A blanket covered his legs. His upper body looked strong, muscled.

Jeff urged her inside. The guard followed, keeping the weapon pointed at their backs. Tessa imagined a big, round target taped to her spine.

"Call off your guard dog," Jeff said between clenched teeth.

The man in the wheelchair smiled slightly. "Emil is here for my protection." He gestured with his hand, and Emil lowered his weapon and stepped back.

Tessa had no doubt Emil could swiftly raise the rifle and shoot them both before they could get out of the way.

"What do you intend to do with us?" Jeff asked.

"That all depends on you, Agent Steele."

"You were waiting for us," Jeff stated. "Your men at the lake missed on purpose."

The man inclined his head. "That is correct."

"To what end?" Jeff pressed.

"Please, let's not discuss business standing here in the entryway." He gripped the wheel handles, spun his chair and rolled down a hallway. "Come, have some tea."

She shared a curious and concerned glance with Jeff. At least they weren't being taken into the woods and killed, but what kind of drug lord in the Pacific Northwest invited prisoners into his home for tea? Instead of being reassured, she felt nervous and tense.

The hallway led to a dining room. A large round table with Queen Anne–style chairs dominated the middle of the room. A curio cabinet filled with brightly colored blown glass sculptures was against the back wall. Brocade curtains gathered back by braided cord hung over large windows that let in the late-afternoon sunlight.

A rolling cart held a silver tea service with three gold-rimmed teacups. The setting seemed incongruous with the man in the wheelchair. Big-boned and unshaven, he was far from refined. His fingers, too thick for the teacup's handle, were better suited to hard labor than holding a delicate piece of china.

"Who are you?" Tessa asked.

"Sherman Roscha's the name," their host replied.

"You run this marijuana farm," Jeff stated.

Sherman narrowed his gaze briefly on Jeff. "Have a seat, and I'll explain."

"Could we wash up first?" Jeff held his hands out, showing the dirt and grime covering his fingers and palms.

Tessa had been trying hard not to think about the germs and bacteria coating their hands, but now she frowned down at her fingers. Her nails were chipped, and dirt was embedded in the creases of her skin and under her nails.

"Of course, where are my manners?" Their host waved for Emil to step forward. "Take them to their rooms."

"Rooms?" Jeff asked.

"Until I decide what to do with you, you'll be my guests."

"How hospitable of you," Jeff said, his tone brimming with sarcasm.

A loud banging at the door startled Tessa, and Jeff tucked her close to his side.

"Take care of that," Sherman instructed Emil.

Emil shot them a ferocious glare before disappearing down the hall. The front door opened.

"I need to speak to him!"

Tessa flinched at the familiar male voice, but she couldn't place where she knew it from.

"He's busy." Emil's rough tone made Tessa shiver.

"I don't care. Uncle! Uncle Sherman!"

There was the sound of a scuffle, and then the door shut. Muffled shouting made it clear the man wasn't going away quietly.

Beside her, Jeff tensed.

"I can see your mind whirling, Agent Steele. My guard is gone. Can you overpower a hapless cripple and escape with the lovely doctor?" Sherman's thin lips spread into a humorless smile. From beneath the folds of the blanket covering his lap, he produced a handgun. "I assure you, I'm a good shot. You'd be dead before you took two steps." Sherman shook his head. "And that would leave the poor doctor alone and defenseless."

Tessa curled her fingers around Jeff's and squeezed, hoping he'd get her message not to try anything. She had no doubt Sherman wouldn't hesitate to shoot.

Emil returned, went to his boss's side and leaned down to whisper in Sherman's ear.

Anger flashed in the older man's eyes.

"Take them to their rooms while I deal with my nephew."

Emil jerked his head toward a hallway, clearly indicating they were to precede him. Jeff placed his hand at the small of her back and urged her forward.

At the first closed door, Emil said, "This is the doctor's."

Jeff pushed the door open. Tessa leaned around him to peer into the room. The walls were a lovely shade of blue, white lace curtains hung over the two windows and a matching lace coverlet lay over a queen-size bed. A plush velvet chair in a deep indigo sat by the window with a stack of books, creating a reading corner. A door next to an armoire led to a private bath.

"Whose room is this normally?" she asked Emil.

Sadness darkened his eyes. "It was Katherine's. But she's gone."

Katherine meant something to Emil. The moment of vulnerability gave Tessa hope the man wasn't as bad as he appeared. "Who was she?"

He lowered his voice; apparently, even this

scary man used caution when it came to Sherman. "Sherman's wife. She was a great lady. She founded this camp as a refuge for runaways like me."

Which explained Emil's loyalty. Keeping her voice low, she asked, "What happened to her?"

His eyes took on a faraway look. "Cancer. She moved into this room when it got real bad to shelter Sherman and the kids from her pain. But we all saw it. That's when he planted the crops of cannabis and built the production warehouse."

Visibly pulling himself back from whatever memories had surfaced, he shook his head as if realizing he was saying too much. His gaze hardened, and he pointed to the next door. "That's yours," he said to Jeff.

Jeff's concerned eyes met hers. She didn't like the idea of being separated, either. With Jeff, she felt safe. Alone, she was vulnerable.

"I'm staying with her," Jeff said, crossing his arms over his chest.

"No," Emil said and shoved Jeff down the hall, then used the barrel of the rifle to make his point, literally jabbing the thing into Jeff's gut.

Fearing Jeff would do something to provoke Emil into firing, she said, "It's okay, Jeff. We're right next door to each other."

With one last look at Jeff, she stepped into the room and shut the door. A moment later, it was locked from the outside. She shivered. On the one hand, this was a million times better than the toolshed, but she was still a prisoner.

How long would it be before they were killed? Because there was no way Sherman could release them now that they knew who he was and what he and his people were up to. What sort of game was he playing?

The windows in the room Jeff had been imprisoned in were nailed shut. The door locked from the outside. Frustrated, he washed up, marveling that there was plumbing in the house. Though Sherman didn't seem the roughing-it type.

Jeff searched the bath and bedroom for something to use as a weapon or a means of escape and found nothing but a change of clothes on the chair in the corner. The lamp had been bolted to the nightstand and didn't even have a cord that he could use to his advantage.

A half hour after being shoved into the room, the door was unlocked and pushed open. Emil and Tessa stood in the hall.

Emil gestured with his gun. "Boss is waiting."

Glad to see Tessa unharmed, Jeff bit back the sharp reply that the boss could keep waiting. Joining Tessa in the hall, he noted she'd changed into a fresh pair of jeans and a long-sleeved blouse and had washed the dirt away from her face and hands. She looked fresh and pretty but her amber-colored eyes were filled with apprehension.

Taking her hand, Jeff gave her a reassuring squeeze. Somehow, someway, he would find a way out of this situation for both of them.

Back in the dining room, Sherman waited at the table in his wheelchair. Emil took a post behind Sherman, his rifle held at the ready. A white tablecloth covered the dark wood table along with service for three. Tessa took the seat to Sherman's right. Jeff ignored the place setting on Sherman's left and sat in the chair beside Tessa.

Sherman arched an eyebrow. "It's nice to see how protective you are of the lovely doctor."

Jeff's teeth ground together. He hated that he'd revealed his vulnerable point to Sherman, who no doubt would use Jeff's weakness to his advantage. Jeff needed to figure out Sherman's agenda and Achilles' heel to even the playing field.

"You said you'd explain," Jeff prompted.

"Yes, I did, didn't I?" Sherman poured tea from a silver pot and slid the cup to Tessa. "Tea, Agent Steele?"

"No, I don't want tea. I want answers."

"Of course you do." Sherman motioned with his hand, and a man stepped into the room.

The same man who'd captured them in the woods. Tall and lanky with brown hair falling to his shoulders and a five-o'clock shadow darkening his jaw. His cold, lizardlike eyes were trained on Tessa and gleamed with male interest. Jeff's blood boiled. He very deliberately placed his arm around the back of her chair, his hand resting lightly on her shoulder. She shot him a grateful glance while sipping her tea.

"This is Aaron. He's my right hand," Sherman said. "And my legs." Sherman let out a mirthless laugh.

Aaron took the seat Jeff had snubbed. He poured himself tea and added two sugars before saying, "Welcome to Camp Sherman."

The insincere words grated on Jeff's nerves. He turned his attention to the man Kyle called the boss. "You didn't bring us here for relaxation," he said. "Why are we here?"

Aaron pointed a finger at Tessa. "Unfortunately, we need her help."

"My help?" Tessa set her cup down abruptly. Liquid sloshed onto the table, the dark tea staining the white cloth cover.

"Yes," Sherman said. "Killing the fish in the lake was never our intent."

"What about the people you hurt?" Jeff asked.

Sherman shrugged. "Again, not our intent." He turned his gaze to Tessa. "We need your help to figure out the right insecticide to use for the plants that won't harm the wildlife."

"And you couldn't just ask for help?" Tessa mopped up the spilled tea with a paper napkin.

Aaron snorted. "We couldn't very well let anyone know we're here, now, could we?"

Which was why the shooters had forced him and Tessa into the woods. But did they intend to let them leave? No. Sherman and his henchmen had no intention of letting them go.

Tessa tapped Jeff's leg. She'd obviously connected the same dots he had. No one knew where she or Jeff had disappeared to and would probably never know. Once Sherman and his men had what they wanted from Tessa, she and Jeff were as good as dead. Their bodies would be buried somewhere deep in the forest or left out for bear food.

They needed to play this out and pray God would provide an opportunity to escape.

*How strong is your faith?*

Tessa's words replayed themselves in Jeff's head.

His fingers curled around hers. He had nothing but faith to go on here. Would it be enough?

"And if I don't help you?" Tessa dreaded the answer.

Sherman exchanged a glance with Aaron.

"Then we'll have to find someone else who will help us."

She shivered at the implied threat in his words. If she didn't help, she was of no use to them. And if she was of no use to them, they might as well kill her and Jeff now and possibly kidnap her colleagues. She couldn't let that happen. She'd do what she could to buy Jeff time enough to figure out a way for them to escape.

His strong, capable hand held hers, comforting and sure.

Maybe she was placing too much trust in him. Too much faith. He was only a man after all. One man with no weapon. And she was the means to keep him in line so he wouldn't force a confrontation and end up with a bullet in his heart.

But Jeff believed in God. Believed that God would protect them.

What if Jeff was wrong? What if faith wasn't enough? What if they were doomed no matter what they did?

Despair threatened to paralyze her. She shook it off. As long as there was breath in her body, she had a chance at survival.

If helping Sherman and company figure out their insecticide problem bought her and Jeff time, that was what she'd do. Jeff had said God would expect him to be smart and take action. She assumed that went for her, as well.

"I don't have to see your operation to test the chemical components of the insecticide you're using," she said.

Jeff gave her hand a squeeze. "You could have a bad batch of insecticide. I would guess the operation has been in place a long time."

Sherman nodded. "My great-grandfather settled on this parcel of land before the government gobbled up all the acreage and turned it into a wilderness park. Right where we are now, there used to be a log cabin built by my great-grandfather and my grandfather. But they were kicked off, and the cabin was torn down."

"How did you rebuild without anyone knowing?" Jeff asked. "And build so much?"

"Friends in high places," Sherman replied.

Meaning greased palms and payoffs. Tessa knew that sort of thing happened, but she'd never been faced with the evidence of corruption. "Why?"

Sherman tilted his head. "Why what?"

"Why are you here? Why are you growing marijuana?"

Aaron sat back and crossed his arms over his chest.

"Money. Why else?"

"But there has to be more to it than that," Tessa said. "From what I can tell, you don't live an extravagant lifestyle."

Sherman folded his hands and leaned his elbows on the table. "You are very perceptive, Dr. Cleary. There are many uses for the plants we grow. Not all of them illegal."

"You grow medical marijuana?" she asked. Many states in recent years had legalized small amounts of the substance for medicinal as well as recreational uses. Washington State was one of them. But Sherman's expansive operation was on government land and yielded more than the regulations of grows allowed.

"We do. Much of what we grow is the plant Blue Dream of the *sativa* species of cannabis. It doesn't have as heavy an effect as the more potent *indica* species, but it is efficient for medicinal purposes." With a nod to Aaron, he added, "And lucrative."

"Very," Aaron agreed.

"Take Dr. Cleary and Agent Steele to the warehouse," Sherman said.

Aaron's lips pressed together, clearly not wanting to do as his boss instructed. Sherman arched an eyebrow. Finally, he pushed back from the table. "Come on."

Jeff rose and offered her his hand. She appreciated his manners even in this stressful situation and had to admit she felt safer when she held his hand.

They left the small house and walked with Aaron to the warehouse.

"Why are there no women here?" she asked, again noting the lack of visible females.

Aaron paused, his dark eyes glinting in the waning sunlight. "Too much of a distraction."

His gaze ran the length of her, sending a chill of revulsion rippling in its wake. She pressed closer to Jeff, thankful for his steady presence. She sent up a silent prayer of gratitude. If Jeff hadn't insisted on accompanying her, she'd be here alone.

"This is where the plants are harvested."

Aaron held open the door to the warehouse and gestured for Tessa and Jeff to enter.

Tessa hesitated before stepping through the doorway. Like Alice stepping through the looking glass, Tessa feared she wouldn't be able to return from the trip inside the workings of Sherman's marijuana grow.

"It's harvest time," Aaron stated, leading them inside. "When the white pistils turn brown or red, depending on the species, we cut the stalks and hang them to dry." He pointed to the many leafy plants hanging upside down from racks in the ceiling.

Long tables had been set up, and two dozen men sat on stools, clipping the larger leaves from the stalks, until only the buds remained. She met the gaze of the young man who'd brought them their food. Kyle looked away and continued to work, using the small shears to nip away at the plant in his hands. There were several stray sets of scissors left unattended on the tables, their sharp points attracting her attention.

"They are doing what we call scissor work," Aaron explained. "Clipping the water leaves off and shaping the buds."

As Aaron moved farther away and continued to explain the harvesting process to Jeff, Tessa pretended interest in the Christmas-tree-shaped product lying on silk screen trays. She stepped close to a thin, sickly-looking man in his mid-to late-thirties.

Using Aaron's theory that females distracted, she leaned a hip against the table and peered at the man while her hand rested on top of a small set of clippers with a blue handle. "You don't look well. Are you okay?"

He jerked his head up, his blurry-eyed gaze startled as if he'd only now realized she was there. "Uh, yeah, uh, I'm okay."

"Dr. Cleary," Aaron called, "please don't disrupt their work. We have a schedule to keep."

Her hand tightened around the clippers. She moved away from the table and jammed her hands into the pockets of her jeans, then subtly untucked her blouse so it hung over the pocket, concealing the scissors. Rejoining Jeff and Aaron, she prayed like crazy she could keep the small shears hidden until she could figure out how to use them to escape.

# SIX

Jeff stared at Tessa with a wave of curiosity cresting over his determination to keep his expression neutral. The extra tension on her lovely face alerted him that she was up to something. She gave him a tight smile and clutched his arm, pressing into his side.

Something hard jabbed into his hip.

With her gaze on Aaron, she shifted her shirt to the side. The head of a pair of clipping shears poked out of her jean pocket. Pride and admiration flared bright in his chest.

The woman was even more resourceful and brave than he'd first imagined. He liked that. Liked her, which only made him more determined to somehow get them out of this situation in one piece.

"Take them," she whispered.

As much as he'd like to palm the scissors for later use, he wouldn't take away her only weapon. "Keep them," he whispered back. "Just in case."

She looked at him with a questioning frown.

Jutting his chin toward Aaron, he whispered, "Go for the throat."

Her lovely eyes widened as the meaning in his words sank in. A visible tremor rippled through her.

Aaron glanced over his shoulder, his eyes narrowed. "Get a move on it."

Tessa adjusted her shirt over the shears. Jeff kept her close. For her protection, he told himself. Though he couldn't deny how right it felt having her melded to his side as if they belonged together. Which they didn't.

There was no future where they ended up together. If—no, when—they got out of this mess, they both had careers to return to.

But he would do everything in his power to ensure they *had* a future.

Aaron led them to the rear of the warehouse and out the back door, stopping at another toolshed. This one housed the insecticide spray cans right next to a large water pump. Several hoses fed out of the pump and through a hole in the back of the toolshed.

Tessa pointed. "Well, there you go."

Jeff scoffed, "I get *genius alert* when I see those two things together."

The corners of Tessa's mouth curled into a smile at his sarcastic tone.

"One of these hoses leads to the irrigation system," Jeff said, remembering the piping they'd seen running along the ground providing water to the stalks of marijuana they'd found. "The pump must be attached to a water source."

"Very good, Agent Steele," Aaron mocked. "You get the gold star." He barked out a vicious laugh. "Oh, wait, you already have one." He reached across and ripped the badge from Jeff's shirt.

A rush of anger crashed through Jeff, making his fingers curl into a fist. The guy didn't know a star from a shield. Seeing his badge in Aaron's filthy hands made Jeff's blood boil.

Tessa grabbed hold of his hand as if she feared he'd retaliate. He held perfectly still. He was smart enough to pick his battles.

"You're taking lake water and then replenishing it with the tainted water," Tessa said. "That's how the toxin is getting into the lake."

Aaron snorted. "The lake's too far away. There's a stream fifty yards northeast."

"Which runs into the lake," Jeff pointed out, though he was unable to keep scorn from lacing his words.

Aaron made a disdainful face. Obviously, the guy didn't care one way or the other that they were poisoning the water and causing harm to both nature and humans.

Tessa released her hold on him to examine the labels on the insecticide cans. Her eyebrows bunched together in apparent puzzlement. "Is this the only pest control you use?"

Aaron shrugged. "As far as I know."

"Don't you oversee the operation?" Jeff asked.

Narrowed dark eyes bore into Jeff. Tension crackled off Aaron like live electricity. The AK-47 hanging from a strap across his chest shifted as his hand closed over the grip. "You calling me a liar?"

Tessa's hand clamped on Jeff's arm in silent warning. He clenched his jaw shut, biting back a reply that could potentially get them killed.

"This is neem oil," Tessa said quickly. "It's a naturally occurring pesticide found in the seed of the neem tree. It wouldn't cause the toxicity that I found in the dead fish."

"What about people?" Jeff asked, diverting his attention away from Aaron.

"Some skin irritation if directly exposed. Maybe digestive issues if swallowed."

*But not respiratory distress.* The unspoken words hung in the air.

There was something else at play here. Some other substance invading the flow of liquid streaming down the mountain slope to the lake. But what?

"Could something else have been added to the neem oil?" Jeff asked.

"It's possible." She turned to Aaron. "I need my sample kit from my duffel bag. I can at least test what's here to see if it has a different chemical component to it."

Aaron stared at her for a moment before curling his lip. "You can ask Sherman about that."

Jeff sensed there was some animosity between the two men.

Aaron shut the doors to the shed. "Let's go."

He escorted them toward the main house. Jeff stared at the greenhouse. Several men exited. One looked their way. Tessa let out an audible gasp. Jeff sent her a questioning glance. Aaron must have heard her, as well, because he whipped his gaze to her.

"Twisted my ankle. Loose rock," she said hastily and produced a sudden limp. Then pointed to the greenhouse. "What are you growing in there?"

"More of the same," Aaron muttered, nudging Jeff in the kidney with the barrel of his rifle.

"You're using hydroponic growing," Jeff said.

Aaron grunted but kept poking Jeff to keep him walking.

"I've heard of hydroponics but have never seen it," Tessa said, keeping pace while playing up her imaginary limp. Jeff wondered what had her so freaked out.

"The plants are grown in an inert growing

medium, like rock wool or clay, rather than soil. The plants are fed with a nutrient-rich solution. It gives the grower more control of the harvest time and yield," Jeff explained.

"We should look in there, too," Tessa said.

"It's off-limits," Aaron snapped just as they reached the house where Sherman and Emil waited for them on the porch.

"You know a thing or two about our business, agent man," Aaron said.

"It's not rocket science," Jeff shot back. But everything relating to the growth, processing and distribution of drugs did play a huge role in a border agent's workday. It was his job to know a thing or two.

"Maybe not, but it does require some chemistry and dedication," Sherman said. "Thank you, Aaron."

Aaron grunted and walked away. Once he was out of earshot, Jeff said, "The insecticide used for the plants isn't the cause of the toxin." He pointed to the greenhouse. "We need to look in there."

"I'd like to see the hydroponic system you have," Tessa chimed in.

"I'd like to show it to you," Sherman said

with a smile aimed at Tessa. He grabbed the wheels of his chair and rolled toward the ramp.

Emil stepped in front of Sherman, forcing the older man to brake. Sherman frowned. "What is it?"

"Going into the greenhouse is not a good idea," Emil said. "Aaron keeps a tight rein on the product in there."

"Who runs this organization?" Sherman asked, his voice deadly soft.

"You, sir," Emil said.

"That's right." Sherman waved Emil out of the way. "It's about time I looked in on things in the greenhouse. Dr. Cleary, Agent Steele, come along."

Emil moved aside, but the uneasy expression on his normally stoic face sent Jeff's senses on high alert. Something about the greenhouse upset the enigmatic Emil enough to speak against his boss.

Keeping Tessa close, Jeff hurried them after Sherman, who wheeled his chair with swift, strong arms.

"We built the greenhouse to attempt a new method of growing," Sherman explained.

"Personally, I'm good with the product we're producing the old-fashioned way. But progress is progress. It's become a competitive business."

The greenhouse wasn't fitted with a ramp like the rest of the compound. Emil reached past Sherman to open the door, then he grabbed the handles of the wheelchair and maneuvered Sherman into the greenhouse. Jeff let Tessa precede him. When he stepped inside, the enclosed humidity hit him in the face. The low hum of the water pump echoed off the frosted windows. Bright lights bathed tall plants in a warm glow. A dozen men froze and stared at Sherman before slinking into the shadows. One man fled out the back door.

A short, younger man bustled forward. His nervous glance bounced from Sherman to Emil and back to Sherman. "Sir, can we help you?"

"Carl, Dr. Cleary needs to see what you are feeding the plants," Sherman said.

"Of course," Carl said. "We use the best nutrient solution there is."

He led them to a corner cabinet. Tessa inspected the boxed solution. Her eyebrows pinched together. "I don't get it. This looks to be in order. But I'd need my test kit to be sure."

Two of the workers had moved to stand side by side in front of a large section of plants. Their anxious expressions stirred Jeff's internal alarm system. What were they trying to hide?

Jeff shimmied past a row of tall marijuana plants and stepped closer. The two men shifted nervously. Glancing past the taller guy's shoulder, Jeff noticed that the marijuana plants in this section were raised on trays and underneath were containers filled with different types of foliage.

The guy blocked his view. Jeff pushed him out of the way.

"Hey!"

"Agent Steele, what are you doing?" Sherman called out.

Emil stalked toward Jeff but Jeff paid him no heed, his attention on the containers. He recognized the spiky leaves of the damiana and the fuller leaves of *Althaea officinalis,* the plant that marshmallows originally came from.

Both herbs were used in the production of a

synthetic street drug. When dried, the plants were laced with a chemical version of tetra-hydrocannabinol, JWH-018, which worked on the same receptors in the brain as marijuana. Only problem was the new drug was more potent. Lethal. And illegal in all fifty states. His chest tightened with dread.

Spying a spray jug, he grew angry. Every instinct told him it would contain the chemical JWH-018. "Tessa." He held the jug up for her to see.

She took the jug and smelled the contents. She drew back, her nose wrinkling. "Phew. That's it."

Sherman wheeled forward. "What is this?"

Jeff didn't trust the puzzlement on Sherman's face. "Your man Aaron is making synthetic marijuana passed off as an inhalable incense, otherwise known as Spice, K2, Mr. Nice Guy and a variety of other names." Jeff set the spray jug down. "This stuff has caused numerous deaths and a whole host of serious side effects ranging from full psychosis to heart attacks to breathing problems as we saw in the lake swimmers."

"I didn't authorize this," Sherman said.

Jeff turned his gaze on the tall man. "Where do you do the drying and packaging of this stuff?"

The guy clamped his lips together and remained mute.

"Sean, tell Agent Steele what he wants to know!" Sherman barked. "Don't concern yourself with Aaron. He'll answer to me."

The guy hesitated as if trying to decide who he was more afraid of: Sherman or Aaron. Finally, he said, "We process it in the cabin marked *Spetsii*."

Sherman's lip curled. "Which is ironic, since *spetsii* is Russian for *spice*."

The front door of the greenhouse banged open. Aaron stomped in. The thundercloud rolling across his face sent unease sliding down Jeff's spine. Though Sherman was a crook for growing illegal marijuana on government land, he didn't strike Jeff as a cold-blooded killer. Aaron, on the other hand…

"I told you this was off-limits," Aaron said as he stormed in along with a blast of cooler air. He'd replaced the rifle with a handgun that now was aimed in their direction. He pulled up short when he saw Sherman.

"Aaron." Sherman spun the chair. "Do you have any idea what you've done? Because of you, our operation has become vulnerable to discovery."

A mulish expression settled on Aaron's broad face as he lowered the weapon. "You said I could grow what I wanted in here."

"I meant any species of cannabis, not make a designer drug that kills. Nothing grabs the law's attention quicker than people dying," Sherman shouted. "Emil, relieve Aaron of his weapon and have two guards escort him to his cabin and keep him there."

"Come on, you can't do this," Aaron sputtered.

Emil nodded, took the weapon from Aaron and stepped outside.

Aaron sent Jeff and Tessa a furious glare. "I should have killed you when I had the chance."

"Enough," Sherman said, his voice low.

Two guards entered. Each took a side and walked Aaron out the door.

Sherman shook his head, remorse filling his eyes. "That boy will be the death of me yet. If his mother were alive she'd have boxed his ears for pulling a stunt like this."

"He's your son?" Tessa asked quietly.

With a sigh, Sherman rolled the chair to where he could face them. "Yes. He's my son. He royally messed up. But we'll make this right. I can't undo the damage done to the lake, but I can guarantee there won't be any more harmful chemicals flowing down the mountain." He wiped a hand over his jaw. "I want to help people. People like me who are in constant pain."

"Then why didn't you move your operation and become a legal grower when the law changed?" Tessa asked.

"I have too much invested here. There are over ten thousand plants spread through the forest. Besides, I already told you, my family was on this land before the government came in and took it away."

"What about us?" Jeff asked. Now that they were no longer needed to find the source of the toxin, their chances of getting out of the forest alive were plummeting fast.

With a regretful twist of his lips, Sherman

said, "I'm sorry to say that I can't let you leave. You're a liability."

Jeff's mind scrambled for a way to get Tessa out of this situation. He said the only thing that came to mind that he thought Sherman would be interested in. "What if you had a Border Patrol agent in your back pocket?"

Beside him, Tessa gasped.

He couldn't afford to glance her way to reassure her that he wouldn't betray his oath to his country. Border agents were guardians of the United States of America's borders. Jeff took that very seriously.

He was a part of the frontline of this nation's defense, protecting the public from terrorists and instruments of terror, both foreign and domestic.

And though what Sherman was doing may not seem like an act of terror, he was hurting the people Jeff swore to protect with vigilance, integrity and professionalism. He would do whatever it took to fulfill his vows.

But there was no way for Tessa to know that he was bluffing. She didn't know him or trust him enough. Regardless, he had to sell this story to Sherman if he was going to make sure she left this place alive and in one piece.

Tessa stared at Jeff with a mix of horror and confusion. He couldn't be serious. Jeff wouldn't throw out his principles to work for Sherman's illegal organization. This had to be some sort of ploy.

Yes, she decided. Jeff was trying to gain Sherman's trust so they could use that to escape. Her mind refused to accept that he'd betray her or his country. But she couldn't say that about the man she'd seen earlier coming out of the greenhouse.

Ranger Randy. The young park ranger who'd picked her up from the airport had been among the men leaving the greenhouse. Now she knew why the voice of the man who'd called Sherman his uncle had sounded familiar. Randy was Sherman's nephew.

She'd met Randy's gaze, and he'd furtively touched a finger to his lips. Evidently, he wanted her to keep from acknowledging him. Why?

She needed to locate him, talk to him and discover if he was friend or foe.

Sherman stroked his chin. "Hmm, now, that's an intriguing idea."

"Isn't it, though?" Jeff said, his voice taking on a coaxing tone. "Think about it. You've gone undetected for a long time, but now you'll be on the radar thanks to Aaron's carelessness. This whole area will be under suspicion. I can make that suspicion go away."

"And just how do you propose to do that?" Sherman asked.

Tessa wanted to know that, as well.

Jeff's smile was sly and so unlike the man she'd come to know over the past few days that she took a step back.

"I'll spin a story. Give me a backpack full of spice and a jug of the synthetic THC and I'll say we found them abandoned on the shore. The chemicals leaked into the lake."

"You think you could pull that off?" Sherman said, doubt filtering through his tone.

"Yes," Jeff said, appearing full of confidence. "For a price."

Barking out a laugh, Sherman pointed a finger at him. "Ah, here it is. What price?"

"Ten percent of the profits, and we keep our mouths shut and the authorities away."

Sherman turned his sharp-eyed gaze on her. "From the look on the doctor's face, I don't think she's on board with this idea, Agent Steele."

"Then she can stay here," Jeff said, his voice hard. "Her choice."

Tessa swallowed back the bile clogging her throat as both men stared at her. She met Jeff's gaze. His flinty blue eyes regarded her steadily. There was no give in his gaze or his expression. Confusion swirled within her. She prayed this was an act. A very convincing one.

Sherman's chuckle broke the tension crackling in the air.

"I'll take your proposition under advisement, Agent Steele." Sherman shifted in his chair and grimaced. Lines of pain gathered around the edges of his eyes and pinched the corners of his mouth. "Time to return to the house."

Empathy stirred beneath her breastbone. It was obvious Sherman's condition caused him great agony, but that didn't excuse what he was doing.

As they walked across the compound, once

again heading toward the house that acted as their prison, Tessa sought Jeff's attention. She wanted to tell him about Ranger Randy.

Jeff, however, wasn't cooperating. He kept his gaze ahead and refused to respond to her tugging prompts to gain his notice. When they entered the house, he walked straight to his room and shut the door. Emil cast her a speculative glance as he locked Jeff inside.

Curling her fingers into fists, Tessa moved into the room she'd been given and waited as Emil locked the door from the outside.

Had she been wrong about Jeff?

Had he seen an opportunity for personal gain, and was he ready to exploit it?

She hated to believe that.

She clung to the thought that he was working some angle. But a lingering doubt filled her mind. What if she were wrong about him?

The desire to punch something or someone rose on a tide of anger. She wasn't one usually prone to violence. She clenched her fists until they ached. Desperate to escape this prison, she'd already searched every inch of the room. The windows were nailed shut, and she didn't know how to pick a lock.

Frustrated with the helpless, useless despair overwhelming her, she sank onto the bed. Taking deep breaths, she fought for control of the panic welling up from deep within her.

A tear slid down her cheek. Who was she kidding? She had no control over this situation. She had no control, period. Never had. Not over whether her parents loved her enough to stay together. Not over whether Michael loved her enough to accept her as she was. Not over Jeff's actions.

She had to trust Jeff was the man she hoped he was. But more than that she had to trust God. Because ultimately, He was the only one in control. She sank to her knees. "Oh, God, please, help us."

A tapping sound pulled Tessa from her fervent prayers. The room was shrouded in darkness. Beyond the window, day had slipped to night. She'd been praying so intently for a long time and hadn't noticed the encroaching night. A chill skated down her spine. The temperature in the room had dipped, as well. She reached for the bed covering.

*Tap, tap, tap.*

She froze and stared at the window. A face appeared. Her heart slammed against her ribs. She clamped a hand over her mouth to stifle the scream clawing up her throat.

Ranger Randy.

She scrambled off the floor and hurried to the window. She mimed that the window had been nailed shut. He nodded. Waved her back, then quickly and efficiently—like he'd done this before—covered the whole window with duct tape, leaving a small hole in the center.

Randy tapped the center point with a small metal tool. A spiderweb of cracks soundlessly spread across the glass but didn't fall. Randy removed the entire window in seconds. She was impressed. And stoked to have a way out of the bedroom.

"Grab a blanket and throw it over the sill," Randy instructed in a whispered tone.

Tessa yanked the bed cover off the bed and tossed it over the exposed edges of broken glass in the windowsill.

"Come on," he whispered. "We don't have much time."

With Randy's help, she climbed out. When her feet hit the ground, her right boot heel hit the edge of a stone and she wobbled. She'd have to be more careful. She couldn't injure herself now when they were so close to escaping.

Randy gripped her elbow and tugged her away from the house.

"I can't leave Jeff," she said, forcing him to stop. "We have to break him out, too."

Randy frantically searched the darkness. "No time."

"Either we break him out, or I'm not going."

"He's not worth it," Randy said. "I heard he wants to work for Sherman."

"Don't you work for him?" she shot back in a whispered rush.

"He's my uncle. I don't have a choice," he whispered back. "In my family, blood is thicker than anything else."

"Even polluted water and sick people?"

"Yes."

"Then why are you helping me?"

Scrubbing a hand over his jaw, he whispered, "I don't know. They went too far by kidnapping you two."

"All the more reason we have to break Jeff out," she pressed.

Randy sighed. "Fine, but we gotta hurry." They rushed to the brightly lit window of Jeff's room.

Crouched down in the shadows beneath the window, Randy said, "We're too exposed. He's got to turn off his light."

Taking the risk of being seen by anyone watching the back of the house, she stretched to her full height and peeked into the room. Jeff paced in front of the door. She rapped her knuckles on the glass. His head turned in her direction. His eyes widened with surprise, then narrowed to disbelief. He rushed to the window. She pointed to the overhead light. He nodded and quickly crossed the room to flip the switch, throwing the room into darkness.

Randy jumped up and did the duct-tape trick to the window until all the pieces of glass broke out. Within minutes, Jeff climbed out the empty windowpane.

"Hurry," Randy whispered urgently and ran toward the woods.

Tessa raced after him, aware of Jeff right on her heels. Once they were a good distance from the compound, Jeff grabbed her by the arm and spun her around.

"What do you think you're doing?" Though his voice was hushed, there was no mistaking the anger in his tone.

"Rescuing you," she shot back, irritated by his lack of gratitude.

With a growl, he pulled her tight against his chest and lowered his head to capture her lips with his.

Shock stole her breath. Her mind exploded with multicolored stars. Her hands gripped his shoulders, her fingers flexing, digging into his biceps as she returned the kiss with all she was worth.

"Excuse me," Randy interrupted. "There's no time for this!"

Jeff broke the kiss. Tessa blinked up at him. Though she could barely see his face in the shadows, she was sure he was grinning, and then they were running back into the dark, dense forest.

She only hoped no one followed.

# SEVEN

Running through the forest at night without any guiding light wasn't one of Jeff's favorite activities. He tightened his hold on Tessa, one arm wrapped around her waist, steadying her as she stumbled over an exposed root. The last thing they needed was a sprain or worse. But he'd carry her in a heartbeat if that was what it took to get her to safety.

"Why did you do that?" she asked in a hushed whisper.

"Do what?" he whispered back, though he had a pretty good idea she wasn't talking about him helping her navigate the dark forest. He removed his arm from around her waist but cupped her elbow in his palm.

"Kiss me."

That was what he thought. "We're running

for our lives. You really want to have that discussion now?"

She let out an exasperated noise but ceased asking. Though the light from the moon barely penetrated the thick canopy of towering trees and did little to dispel the gloom of the forest floor, he could see her frustration and her fear. He touched his hand to the small of her back, urging her on.

All around them, the sounds of the night seemed amplified. Birds chirped as they settled for the evening, and an owl hooted high in the trees. Nocturnal crickets created a soothing rhythm broken occasionally by the rustling of some nighttime creature scurrying about, scavenging for food. The thick undergrowth plucked at them like greedy fingers wanting to slow them down. Up ahead, the man leading them deeper into the woods was barely a shadow, tall and lanky, slipping in and out of view. Who was he? Why was the man helping them? Where were they headed?

Why had Jeff given in to the impulse to kiss Tessa?

The questions bombarded him, but he held them at bay, especially that last one. He couldn't let himself dwell on how right and natural it had felt to pull her into his arms, to hold her close, to feel the sweet surrender of her kiss as she clung to him. Or how grateful he'd been to see her face in the window, to know she'd had a chance to escape and leave him behind but hadn't.

She'd risked discovery to free him. His heart expanded in his chest until he thought his rib cage wouldn't be able to contain the emotions flooding through him. All things he could never admit to her.

Taking deep breaths of the pine-scented, earthy forest, he forced himself to stay focused on the here and now. There would be time enough for a Q and A session when they were safe. Just when that would be, Jeff didn't know. First they had to make it out of the forest to someplace where Tessa would be protected.

Then Jeff would do all he could to take Sherman and his illegal drug operation down.

Up ahead, high in a towering tree, a light blinked, catching Jeff's attention. Excitement revved in his blood. "Hey," Jeff called out in a hushed tone.

The man they followed drew up short and spun around. "What?" he asked impatiently.

"The blinking light in that tree," Jeff said, pointing, though he doubted the man could see the gesture. "It's a border camera. I'll climb up and signal for help."

"Nah. Sherman's rigged all the cameras in the forest so they're set on a continuous loop."

Which was why Homeland Security had no idea that Sherman had built a compound in the middle of the North Cascades woods.

"I can disable it," Jeff insisted in a hushed tone. "That would warrant NSA to send agents to check it out."

"It would also send a message to Sherman and let him know which direction we've taken."

"Where are we going?" Jeff debated the wisdom of trusting him. "We should head back to the lake." They would undoubtedly come across the search party that Jeff was positive was out looking for them right now.

"No way. We'd be caught for sure. We're going north. There's a town about fifteen miles away. And a campground even closer."

Jeff sucked in a sharp breath. "We'll be crossing the international border."

"Yes. The Canadians will help. But we have to keep moving. When Sherman discovers you've escaped, he'll tear these woods apart looking for you. He goes crazy when anyone tries to leave."

"How does he get all those men to come to the compound?" Tessa asked.

"Some answer ads from the classifieds." The guy shrugged. "Others are from the streets. Sherman lures them in with the promise of a job, a warm meal and a clean place to live. But once they are here, they're enslaved. Trapped. Held prisoner. He supplies them with all the weed they want. Most don't try to leave, but occasionally one tries and they are always caught."

Tessa rubbed her arms. "What happens to the ones that try to escape?"

"The shed. No food or water. Eventually, they comply and go back to work."

Sherman starved them into submission. Jeff couldn't wait to bring the man to justice. "Has anyone gotten away?"

"Not that I know of." He glanced around as if expecting the armed guards from the compound to materialize from behind the trees. "We need to keep moving."

The man faded into the inky darkness.

"Come on, we don't want to lose him," Tessa said, tugging on his hand.

"Who is he?" Jeff asked.

"Ranger Randy," she said. "He picked me up from the airport and brought me to the ranger station."

"And he's working for Sherman?"

"He's his nephew."

Surprised, Jeff shook his head. More questions rose, but he pushed them back. He increased his speed, urging Tessa along.

Though the air was cold, sweat gathered on Jeff's back, soaking into his shirt.

He became aware of a noise that grew steadily louder the longer and deeper they trekked through the dark forest. The sound triggered recognition. A waterfall.

Aaron had said there was a stream not far from the compound. There were many streams and rivers made by runoff from the glaciers at the peaks of the Cascades, which flowed down through the forest and emptied into the many lakes of the national park.

Including Glen Lake, where Aaron's toxic carelessness had contaminated the water.

Tessa drew to an abrupt halt, forcing Jeff to stop.

"Do you hear that?" she asked in a panicked whisper.

"The waterfall? Yes. It's pretty close."

"No, not that. Listen."

The urgency in her tone prickled his skin. He strained to hear what she had. Filtering out the sound of the waterfall, Jeff heard another noise that sent his heart pounding.

"What are you two doing?" Ranger Randy hustled to their side. "We've got to keep going."

Dread filled Jeff. "Dogs. They have tracking dogs."

Randy cursed. "We have to reach the waterfall, or we're done for." He turned and ran, disappearing into the night.

Gripping Tessa's hand, Jeff urged her to race after Ranger Randy and sent up a desperate prayer for safety.

Tessa struggled to catch her breath. The altitude had increased considerably as they raced through the forest, but it was fear constricting her lungs and throat, making the intake of oxygen difficult. Not even the memory of Jeff's kiss could contain the panic nipping at her heels. She doubted the dogs Sherman used to find them would only nip.

"I didn't see dogs in the compound," Jeff said, sounding winded.

"I didn't, either. But we didn't see that much of the operation."

"Enough to know Sherman and his men are dangerous people. The dogs must be kept close by if they're onto our scent so quickly."

She tightened her hold on Jeff's hand, so thankful for his steady and reassuring presence. Though terror and exhaustion threatened to leech her stamina, she pressed on, drawing strength from the man at her side.

He could easily leave her in the dust. But she could feel his restraint in the way he shortened his steps to accommodate her shorter legs, even though she was at the max of her stride. Running had never been her strong suit. Aerobic dance classes at the gym and ice skating were the ways she stayed fit.

She pushed herself harder. They had to

make it to the waterfall. The closer they came, the more the noise of the rushing water drowned out all other sounds.

"This way!" Randy called from somewhere to their left.

Jeff changed directions. She lurched and staggered to keep up.

"You okay?" Jeff asked, his voice barely discernible over the roar of the waterfall that now had risen to a deafening decibel.

Knowing that even if she yelled back her response he'd never hear her, she squeezed his hand in answer.

They broke through the old-growth forest to the edge of a wide stream. Moonlight danced off churning water and revealed a towering waterfall framed by jagged, moss-covered boulders.

"We have to cross." Randy leaned close to yell in their faces. "It's waist-deep near the base of the waterfall. Once we're on the other side, we'll head due north. There's a campground and ranger station."

Tessa swallowed back a mouthful of anxiety. The cascading water falling into a wide pool and flowing downstream would be icy cold, not to mention the current would be difficult to navigate. Jeff tugged on her hand to gain her attention. He stared at her, his blue eyes almost translucent in the glow from the moon.

"We can do this."

She read his lips more than heard his words. She gave him a trembling smile and nodded.

Randy plunged into the water and waded toward the other side of the stream.

Taking a deep breath, Tessa gave Jeff a thumbs-up sign.

He grinned, approval shining through and making her pulse skitter. She wanted to be brave and courageous for him.

Hand in hand they waded into the plunge pool collecting the cascading falls. Her breath caught in her chest as the freezing water soaked through her boots, her jeans and dug into her skin like icy talons. The shifting sand clutched at her boots. She fought to take each step through the current plucking at her, trying to take her downstream. She prayed none of them fell into the polluted water. It was bad enough it was touching their skin.

The water reached her waist, drenching the lightweight jacket and shirt beneath, sending frozen waves of shock through her system. She shivered. Her legs had gone numb. Ice filled her veins. Every cell seemed to freeze. She was becoming a human Popsicle. She had to look to be sure she still clung to Jeff.

A shout rang through the darkness.

She looked over her shoulder to see men and dogs emerging from the forest. One man raised a rifle.

She froze as a scream built in her chest.

Jeff's arm snaked around her waist and lifted her off her feet, gripping her against his chest to carry her to the stream's bank.

The sound of a rifle shot echoed over the waterfall. Water spit at her where the bullet tore into the stream a few inches from them. Jeff battled the rough current and the loamy earth. They emerged onto the riverbank and crawled up the side of the embankment to solid ground. Randy pulled her from Jeff's arms and pushed her forward.

"Go! Go!" Randy shouted.

Tessa ran, her limbs jerky and awkward, numb from the frigid water. The woods offered cover. She had to make it. They all had to make it.

More gunfire erupted.

A man screamed.

Tessa spun around with her heart in her throat. Randy staggered down the embankment and fell face-first into the rushing water. Jeff lunged for him, but Randy was too far out of reach, his body already swirling away in the rapid current.

Tears blurred Tessa's vision. Jeff raced toward her, looping an arm around her waist and forcing her into the forest.

All around her, trees loomed indistinguishable from each other in her misery. Branches reached out like knives, cutting and ripping through her clothes, her skin. She stumbled over a small shrub. Jeff's hand on her arm kept her upright when she'd have fallen down onto the decaying forest floor.

For what seemed like forever, they ran, her body abused by the forest, her lungs aching, her heart as heavy as her waterlogged boots.

Finally, Jeff pulled her into the hollowed-out remains of a fallen dead tree.

Shivering, she sat as her mind replayed the

image of Randy falling into the frigid water. Was he dead?

A knot of guilt rose up from deep within her soul and constricted her chest. If he hadn't helped them…

"Shhh," Jeff crooned in her ear. He wrapped his arms around her and rubbed some warmth back into her limbs. "Breathe."

"Randy." The word came out on a sob.

"I know, I know," Jeff whispered, his voice reflecting the sorrow and regret she felt. He pressed her head to his chest. His heart beat in a fast staccato against her cheek. She let the rhythm lull her to a dreamlike state where the cold couldn't reach her.

"Hey, hey!" Jeff's voice penetrated through the fog in her brain. "Don't sleep. You need to stay awake."

"So sleepy," she mumbled. Her teeth clattered. Her heart pumped at a sluggish rate. She fought to keep her eyes open. Her limbs had gone numb. And strangely she didn't care.

"It's the cold." Jeff grasped her wrist. Her pulse had slowed, just like her breathing. Even the shivers had slackened. He had to get her to someplace warm and dry where she could shed the wet clothes and shoes. If he didn't, she was at risk of going into shock.

What he wouldn't give right now for her bag of essentials.

But it wasn't only the cold seeping in that was shutting down her system. She was no doubt struggling with witnessing Randy being shot. Jeff would give anything to wipe that memory from her mind, but he couldn't. Only time would lessen the horror of it.

He listened to the forest, straining to hear their pursuers. The waterfall had become a dull roar underscored by the sound of barking. Jeff had to assume Sherman's men had crossed the river and were tracking them. Which meant they couldn't stay within the shelter of this dead tree. It would be only a matter of time, most likely minutes, before they were discovered.

Forcing his numb legs to move, he shifted and got his feet beneath himself. "Come on, sweetheart, we have to keep going."

Tessa shook her head. The tie that had held her red curls back was long gone now. Her hair fell over her face, muffling her voice, "Can't we rest more?"

"No." A sense of urgency niggled at the back of his neck, galvanizing him into action. He slipped his arms under hers and lifted her to her feet. "Just a little farther. Randy said there's a campground not far from here."

Once upright, she swayed. He caught her about the waist. "One foot in front of the other," he coaxed.

His words were meant for her, but he found he needed them, too. His limbs were chilled to the bone. Movement hurt. Each step radiated upward in a spark of pain. But he forced himself to do as he said, put one foot in front of the other.

Had the cold water forced the men and dogs to turn back? Jeff prayed so with every fiber of his being.

Up ahead, through the inky shadows, the dark outline of an out-of-place structure took shape. A small travel trailer nestled amid the trees.

His heart pounded, flooding his system with a burst of adrenaline. Renewed with energy and hope, he swept Tessa up into his arms and carried her to the trailer.

He searched the darkness, looking for the vehicle that had towed the trailer into the forest, but there was nothing, only trees and bushes. But someone had driven this trailer here, so that meant a road couldn't be too far away. First, however, his priority was Tessa. He had to risk stopping long enough to get her dry and warm.

He propped Tessa up against the side of the trailer.

"Can you stand on your own?"

"Mmm-hmm," she murmured.

He banged on the metal door. "Hello! Anybody in there?"

Nothing moved. No light came on. He jiggled the handle. Locked. He slammed a fist against the door in frustration. The glass window in the door rattled. He combed the ground for a rock to break the window with.

He found a short, heavy log and rammed it into the glass. It took several tries before the glass gave way. He reached inside the open hole and turned the lock. The door swung open. He verified the trailer was empty.

Tessa slid to the ground. He gathered her in his arms and carried her inside and sat her on the U-shaped bench seat of the dining area. The one-room space was dark and cold. He had to stoop because of the low-lying roofline. He searched the cabinets and found blankets and enough clothes for both of them. He also found a flashlight.

Taking a momentary risk, he turned on the flashlight long enough to assess their surroundings and make sure there were no immediate threats he had to deal with. A small sink and stove gave him hope there was food in the cupboards.

He turned off the light, and while his eyes readjusted to the dark, he wrapped Tessa up in a blanket. She made no noise as she pliantly allowed him to rub her arms, letting the warmth from the friction with the blanket soothe her. "Honey, I need you to stay with me."

"Mmm. 'Kay."

Concern arced through him. He could barely make out her face in the ambient light coming through the broken window. Her pale skin glowed with no color in her cheeks. "I need you to change your clothes."

"What?" she squeaked, rousing a bit.

He opened a door that led to a small bathroom that would barely have enough elbow room to complete her task. "In there." He pushed her inside and then handed her a change of clothes from the cabinet. "You can do it."

She clutched the clothes to her chest. "Are we safe here?"

The scared and vulnerable tone to her voice made his heart contract painfully within his chest. He wished he could reassure her, but he wouldn't lie. "We don't have a choice. If we kept going as we are, drenched and weighted down by our soaked clothes, Aaron would find our dead, frozen bodies. At least warm and dry, we still have a chance to escape."

She accepted his words and shuffled into the bathroom. Jeff shut the door, then quickly changed from his soggy clothes into a pair of well-worn sweats and thermal shirt.

Both were too wide and too short, but he wasn't going to complain. He searched for sustenance and found a box of crackers, a jar of peanut butter and a can of tuna. Not exactly a gourmet feast, but it would do. They needed strength to keep going.

A drawer held a set of plastic utensils. He searched for a knife or screwdriver, anything to use as a weapon. He found a can opener, a plastic spatula, a whisk and a wooden ladle. Useless. Nor could he find any tools with sharp points or edges.

But he did find a jug of distilled water. He tested it to make sure it was really water. It was. He found two plastic cups and poured water into each.

The door of the bathroom clicked open, and Tessa stepped out swaddled in the blanket and oversize sweats and sweat jacket. White socked feet glowed bright poking out the bottom of the blanket.

She shuffled to the cushioned bench seat and plopped down. "Whew. That was exhausting."

His chest filled with affection. Moonlight streamed through the window and touched her like a caress. Her hair was wild and untamed, her eyes wide and dark, and her smile trembled. She'd never looked lovelier to him. The longing to kiss her again gripped him in a tight vise. Forcing his attraction down, he turned his attention to their makeshift meal. He presented his bounty to her on a plate. "This should give us some energy. But we can't linger."

"I've never been so happy to see a saltine before," she said as she picked up the square cracker smeared with peanut butter.

"There's no mayo for the tuna," he said, setting the open can down with two forks.

"That's okay. Mayo isn't good for my figure."

Appreciating the moment of levity, he sat down across from her but angled so that he could keep an eye out the broken trailer window.

She reached over and covered his hand with hers. Her skin was cold, but warmth quickly grew between them. "Thank you for this food."

"God is the one we need to thank." If they hadn't stumbled across this trailer, they'd be as good as dead even before Sherman's men found them.

Her expression grew pensive. "You're right." She lifted her gaze toward the ceiling. "Thank You, God. For everything."

"Amen." Jeff popped a cracker into his mouth.

They ate quickly and silently until it was all gone. Jeff refilled their water. "We should conserve the rest," he said when he noticed the jug was half-gone.

"Agreed." She stacked their plates. "Can we stay here all night?"

"We can only risk a few more minutes. Just because we don't hear the dogs anymore doesn't mean Aaron isn't still tracking us." He took the empty tuna can and plates to the sink. There was no running water, so he wiped them off as best he could with a paper napkin from a stack he'd found.

He stuck the empty tuna can into a plastic bag that had been beneath the sink. No sense in leaving it all out to attract the grizzly or one of the black bears that inhabited the forest. As it was, he owed the owner of the trailer a new window.

When he was finished, he positioned himself by the door, where he could keep a watch out the broken window. Tessa tucked a blanket around him before moving to the bench seat and spreading a blanket over herself. Grateful for her thoughtfulness, he tugged the edges together against the chilled air coming through the opening.

"So are you going to tell me now?" Tessa asked, her voice quiet yet intense.

He knew instantly what she referred to. The kiss. The memory never lingered far from his thoughts.

He studied her face in the soft light streaming into the trailer. She'd tried taming her hair by running her fingers through the curls and tucking them behind her ears. Her high cheekbones created shadows on the landscape of her pretty face.

Raw protectiveness surged through him. If something happened to Tessa, he didn't know if he'd be able to take it. Somehow, in such a short time, he'd come to care about her in a way he hadn't experienced before. She'd squirmed beneath the barricades of his heart, teasing affection and caring into blooming like the winter camellias that would soon be flowering in his mother's garden. How had he let that happen?

No way could he admit to his feelings. He was struggling to come to terms with it all, and revealing his heart wouldn't be a smart move, not when their lives depended on clear thinking. He could pretend not to understand, but she'd see through that ploy. Minimize. That was the way he could deal with her question and the truth of his answer. "What can I say? I was happy to see you. You could have left me there."

"And that's all?"

The question hung in the air. She wanted to know if his feelings for her ran deeper than happiness at being rescued. Whether they did or not didn't matter. Couldn't matter. They were still in danger and on the run for their lives. Confusing the situation with an attraction or infatuation would only complicate everything. Because when they left these woods, they would go their separate ways. That was how it had to be, how he wanted it to be.

"That's it." He could feel her gaze on his back like laser points. Her hurt was a palpable entity that pulsed through the small trailer, making him suddenly claustrophobic. "Let me know when you've warmed up enough to keep moving."

# EIGHT

Tessa burrowed deeper into the blanket covering her. Everything hurt, from her toes to her scalp to her heart.

The faint glow of the moonlight from outside did little to dispel the shadows inside the travel trailer. Jeff had hunkered down by the door, keeping watch. She could hear the sound of his breathing. The rhythmic noise was both reassuring and disconcerting.

The icy night air seeped in through the broken window, chilling her bones despite the dry, oversize sweats and blanket. Drawing her knees to her chest, she berated herself for being upset and disappointed.

Okay, she had reason to be upset. Ranger Randy had been shot, possibly killed, trying to help them escape. The memory of witnessing him tumble into the stream played through her mind. She and Jeff were hiding out in an abandoned travel trailer in the middle of the woods, hoping to evade a madman and his goons. Sherman and his illegal drug-making operation threatened the health of the forest as well as their lives.

Anyone in their right mind would be upset, freaked out and on the edge of panic.

But the disappointment biting at her came from the knowledge Jeff had only kissed her on impulse. He'd said he'd been happy she hadn't escaped without him.

A simple thank-you would have sufficed.

Why had he gone and complicate things with a kiss?

Why was she getting all twisted up inside over a kiss?

It was just a kiss.

Not a promise, not a declaration, not even an "I like you and want to see where this will go" statement.

The kiss didn't mean anything.

It wasn't as if she'd never been kissed before. But somehow this kiss impacted her deeply and stirred in her a yearning for connection in a way she hadn't experienced in a very long time.

But she knew with painful familiarity that opening herself up to connecting with Jeff would only end in heartbreak. Once they escaped these woods—she sent up a quick prayer that they would leave the forest alive—their lives would go separate ways.

And even if there wasn't the matter of distance between them, risking her heart again wasn't something she planned to do, especially with a man who claimed to not believe in love and who wouldn't commit himself to a relationship.

She squeezed her eyes closed with a prayer for safety and for Ranger Randy on her lips. But mostly she prayed for strength. Strength to not only stay alive, but also to keep her heart safe from Jeff.

When she opened her eyes, he looked toward her as if he heard her thoughts. His shadowed gaze made her feel exposed. A blush crept up her neck. She was glad for the inner fire heating her skin but more for the fact he couldn't see the color rising in her face.

"Are you warm?" His gruff voice, his impassive face, gave nothing away.

She swallowed past the dread and resignation clogging her throat. She'd never take a heater for granted again. "As much as I can be."

"We should head out," Jeff said. "That town the younger ranger talked about can't be far."

Sadness enveloped her. "Do you think he's dead?"

Reaching out a hand to help her off the bench, Jeff said, "I don't know. I pray not."

"Me, too."

He held out her shoes. "They're still damp, but they'll have to do."

At least the socks he'd found in the drawer were warm and dry. Forcing her feet into her cold, wet boots worked another chill over her body. She zipped the sweat jacket all the way up, put the hood over her head and tied the string under her chin. Then she wrapped the blanket around herself like a cape.

Jeff found a plastic garbage bag beneath the sink and stuffed their wet clothes inside. "Ready?"

"Yes. Let's get out of here."

"What about the animals?"

"I'd rather take my chances with the four-legged kind than the two-legged ones with guns."

She prayed they didn't encounter either one.

"Wait." He rummaged through the bag of clothes until he found the small set of shears she'd lifted from the warehouse. "Put these in your pocket. They aren't much but that's all we have."

"You should keep them," she insisted.

He shook his head. "If we're caught they'll search me. But they might not search you."

Her hand closed over the scissors with dread. If they were caught. She sent up a plea of protection.

She slipped the shears into the inside pocket of the sweats. The space was meant for a key, not scissors. She pulled the jacket hem down to cover the waistband of the sweats.

Cautiously, Jeff opened the trailer door and poked his head out. "All clear."

Grabbing her hand, he tugged her outside into the moonlight. Here the canopy of trees wasn't nearly as thick, allowing the moon's glow in the cloud-filled sky to illuminate the ground, revealing an overgrown path where a car had once tread, leading away from the trailer. "Let's pray this takes us to safety."

"Amen to that."

He tucked stray curls into the edge of the hood. "Have I told you how impressed I am with you?"

Surprised pleasure curled her cold toes. "No. Are you?"

"Yes." His fingers lingered, lightly tracing her jawline. "When we first met, I pegged you as a pampered, high-maintenance type of female."

A smile tugged at the corner of her mouth. "Oh? What makes you think I'm not?"

"Not many women would hold up so well under the circumstances we've found ourselves in. I'm proud of you."

"Thank you." She inclined her head in acknowledgment, hoping the effect his words had on her didn't show in the shadowed light. She couldn't remember anyone ever saying they were proud of her. Not her parents, not Michael, not her coworkers or boss. Touched to her core, she turned her head to nuzzle his hand. "I wouldn't be doing so well if you weren't here."

He cupped her cheek. "I'm glad I am," he murmured.

"Me, too." Moonlight fell across his well-formed mouth. Longing for him to kiss her again roared through her veins, chasing away the chill that had gripped her moments before. She licked her lips.

On a groan, he captured her mouth with his in exquisite tenderness. She clutched at his shoulders, drawing him closer as yearning and need rose within her, making her forget where they were, making her forget there was no room for romance between them.

She poured all the fear-laden angst and joy-filled hope she could into deepening the kiss. His strong, muscled arms slid around her, crushing her to his solid chest.

There was nowhere she wanted to be more than within his embrace. She melded to him, willingly absorbed by his overwhelming presence.

The kiss ended far too soon but gave her

enough oomph to start down the path tucked beneath the comforting weight of Jeff's arm.

They followed the worn tracks deep into the inky woods with no road in sight. Frustration beat a steady tempo in her head.

Jeff halted abruptly, his body instantly tense.

"What?" she whispered.

"Shh." He hustled her to a thick bramble, shoving her behind him in a protective gesture that endeared him to her in a way no flowers or box of chocolate could ever do.

The thorny branches plucked at the blanket and poked through the material covering her limbs. She clamped a hand over her mouth to keep from making any noise as the sound of men's voices growing louder raised goose pimples on her flesh and sent a wave of fear crashing over her until she thought she'd drown.

"We know you're in there, Agent Steele, Dr. Cleary." Aaron's deep voice assaulted them. "Don't make me destroy the shrubbery. We're taking you back to the compound. Up to you if it's dead or alive."

She dropped her head to Jeff's back. Not

again. They were so close to freedom. Tears of anger and despair pricked her eyes.

He turned to grip her by the arms. "We're sitting ducks in here. We have to give ourselves up."

The moon's glow washed over Jeff's handsome and anxious face. He needed her to be strong. She wanted to be strong, wanted to be the woman he admired. But her legs felt wobbly and her lip quivered. "I know."

"I promise you, I will get you out of this."

She wished she could take comfort in his words, but was too afraid they were doomed and there was nothing either of them could do. "Why has God turned His back on us?"

Jeff shook his head. "God would never abandon us. He'll see us through this."

That was the second time he'd made that claim. She really wanted to believe him.

Anguish threatened to crush her, but she raised her chin, calling on every last ounce of strength she possessed.

"We're coming out," Jeff shouted. "Don't shoot."

Pulling her close, he gave her a quick and purposeful kiss. "Be strong."

She hoped to give him a reassuring smile, but her lips trembled, spoiling the effect. With a nod, he walked out from behind the bushes. Half expecting to be riddled with bullets, Tessa followed. The night suddenly lit up with high-powered flashlights, revealing they were surrounded by a horde of men each with a pair of night-vision goggles hanging around their necks and weapons in their hands. Her mouth went dry.

"Where are your dogs?" Jeff asked, glancing around as if he expected the beasts to charge out of the forest at them.

"Those stupid animals wouldn't cross the stream." Aaron's leering gaze slid over her, leaving a bitter trail of distaste in its wake. "Besides, it was more fun watching you two."

Meaning he and his cohorts had watched them kiss. She fought the urge to gag. Aaron was beyond creepy. Beside her, Jeff's fingers curled into fists. There was no mistaking the anger emanating off him in palpable waves. She feared Jeff would do something to cause Aaron to shoot him on the spot.

She tensed as Aaron stepped up to Jeff and slugged him in the stomach. Jeff doubled over with a grunt of pain. She marveled at Jeff's restraint when he could easily have taken Aaron down, but she knew Jeff well enough now to know with so many guns pointed at them, he wouldn't risk her safety.

She appreciated that even as a scream of rage tore from her. "Leave him alone!"

"That's for making my father doubt me." Aaron's cruel sneer made her stomach curdle. "Bring them."

Two men grabbed Jeff by the arms. A tall, burly man clapped a hand around Tessa's biceps, ripped the blanket from around her and tossed it away before dragging her forward into the trees.

When they reached the edge of the stream, she was hauled through its churning flow. The fast-moving water from the falls plucked at the oversize sweats, threatening to drag her into the current. Only the tight grip of the unshaved man who held on to her kept her from slipping.

On the other side of the stream bank, she noticed drag marks on the ground along with a crimson trail. She bit her lip to keep from tearing up. They'd fished Randy out of the water and thankfully hadn't left him for the coyotes or the grizzly bear to feast on.

The trek back to the compound was longer and more grueling as each step brought them closer to a destiny that made her mind want to shut down. But she couldn't. She would be strong for Jeff. For herself.

Over the noise of the compound's generator, the *whump-whump* of a helicopter filled the woods and sent hope jolting through her. Tilting her neck back, she searched the sky.

If she could see the aircraft, then whoever was inside could see her. The helicopter's shadow passed over them. For the first time she realized there was some sort of material across the compound and attached to the trees like a supersize awning, providing concealment for those on the ground. Her hopes of being spotted sank.

"That's a search party looking for us," Jeff said. "These woods are going to be crawling with agents soon."

Aaron laughed. "Sorry to disappoint you, Agent Steele, but no one will be looking here for you." He pointed to the sky. "From up there, all they see is dense forest. They'll move on. They always do."

Jeff looked up. His jaw tightened. "The camouflage netting won't fool the authorities for long. They'll be back with infrared imaging, and when they do, you're going down."

Aaron's lip curled. "In your dreams. Don't you think we have all contingencies covered?" He tipped his chin to the men on either side of Jeff. "Put him back where he belongs."

"I'm not leaving Tessa," Jeff yelled and struggled against the men trying to lead him away. One of the men struck him on the back of the head with the butt of his weapon. Jeff crumpled into a heap on the hard ground.

"No!" Tessa lurched toward him. The man holding on to her wouldn't let her move. "Please," Tessa pleaded with Aaron. "Don't hurt him."

The malicious glee dancing in Aaron's eyes said there would be no mercy from him.

Helpless to do anything for Jeff, she watched as the men dragged him to the small wooden shed in which they'd first been held captive. They threw him inside and locked the door.

"Take her to my cabin," Aaron told the man holding her.

Horror flooded her. She didn't want to be alone with this fiend. She had no doubt he planned to abuse her before killing her. She dug in her heels and clawed at the hand cinched around her arm. "No! I want to see Sherman."

"That old man won't help you," Aaron said with a wicked gleam in his eyes.

Another man grabbed her other arm.

"Sherman!" Tessa screamed. All around them, men came out of the buildings. Aaron glowered at them, and they slunk back inside.

"Help me! Someone help me!" She continued to kick and scream as the two men dragged her to the first cabin, threw her inside and slammed the door shut.

The square, fixed window in the side of the cabin was the sole source of light in the stark one-room dwelling. A bed, a sink and dresser were the only furniture. She ran to the door and yanked it open. A guard stood there with a rifle, barring her way. There was no compassion, no sympathy for her plight in his flinty eyes. She slammed the door shut.

She had to escape. She looked out the window. Sherman had come out of the house. He and Aaron were arguing. She pounded on the windowpane and screamed for help. If either man heard her cries, they didn't show it.

Pitiful that she'd be turning to the head bad-guy honcho of this illegal operation for help.

Aaron suddenly walked away and stalked toward the cabin. Sherman whirled his wheelchair in the opposite direction and rolled quickly back to his house.

Panic seized her lungs. Her frantic gaze searched for a weapon, something to defend herself with. There was no lamp. She searched the dresser. Nothing but clothes.

She examined the steel-framed bed. Even if she had a screwdriver to work the nuts and bolts keeping the bed together and could use a piece of the frame to defend herself, there was no time. Aaron would be coming through the door any second.

As she straightened, something hard poked her stomach. The scissors. With a trembling hand, she pulled the small tool used to clip the buds from the marijuana stalks from the pocket of her sweatpants. She stared at the instrument in her hands, amazed she hadn't lost them in the forceful current of the stream. Could she use them to protect herself?

Men's voices outside the door jolted her heart into a rapid tempo. Palming the shears so that the sharp, metal tip stuck out between her middle and ring fingers on her dominant hand, she tested the weapon by making a sweeping arc in the air. As weapons went, it wasn't much, but hopefully would work to defend herself with. She prayed it wouldn't come to that.

Jeff came to with a mouth full of blood and dirt.

"About time," a weak male voice spoke from somewhere to his right.

Squinting against the throbbing in his head, he turned to see Ranger Randy sitting propped up against the shed wall. Blood seeped through a bandage covering his thigh. Relief rushed in. "You're alive."

"Yeah, for now," Randy said, his voice low and pain-filled.

Jeff's vision cleared enough to realize

Randy didn't look so good. His pale face beneath his freckles made a cloud look brown. Though he'd survived the gunshot wound to his leg, he was losing blood. The bullet must have nicked an artery. If he didn't get help soon, the wound might still prove fatal.

A spike of panic registered that Tessa was not in the shed. "Where's Tessa?"

He pushed himself to a seated position. The room spun. He held his head for a moment, waiting for the dizziness to abate.

"I heard her screaming." The sorrow in the young ranger's voice sent fear slithering through Jeff like snakes in a pit.

Randy awkwardly rose, leaning heavily on the wall for support. The exertion made sweat pop out on his brow. He stared out the small window in the side of the shed. "They put her in Aaron's cabin."

Terror sank sharp fangs into Jeff's heart. Tessa was in trouble. His promise to keep her safe echoed through his mind. He'd let her down, unable to keep his word.

A fist of self-loathing lodged in his throat. He should have been better prepared. He should have kept them moving last night rather than taking the time to warm up and rest. Failing at the one thing he had sworn to do, protect and serve, weighed heavy on his shoulders.

She didn't deserve what was happening to her. He should have found a way to get them out of the forest long before they were ever caught by Sherman and his men.

Determination to find a way to fulfill his promise to her forced his feet under him. The world swayed, his head throbbed from where he'd taken a hit. He pushed himself to move to the window. Aaron and another man were on the porch of the first small cabin in a row of cabins.

Tessa was inside that room. She would be at Aaron's mercy.

Horrified by what might happen to her, he banged on the window. He couldn't let Aaron hurt her. The glass cracked with the force of each blow. The two men turned toward him. Aaron gestured to the shed, and the man nodded and stalked toward Jeff. Aaron stayed on the porch. Jeff prayed he didn't go inside the cabin. If Aaron harmed Tessa…Jeff clenched his fists.

"When he gets here, then what?" Randy slid down the wall to land on the floor with a thump.

"Can you make it to the door?" Jeff eyed the bright red blood dripping from the saturated bandage on his leg.

Randy grimaced. "I can try."

Jeff needed the man's help. He slid an arm around Randy, lifting him so that he stood on his uninjured leg. Hurrying as best they could, Jeff positioned Randy next to the door. Then he grabbed the water bottle he'd left in the corner and shoved it into Randy's hands. "When he opens the door, untwist the cap. The pressure will make the cap shoot off like a rocket. Aim for his face."

"What are you going to do?

"Disarm him." Hot purpose spread through Jeff's chest. "Then rescue Tessa."

# NINE

Standing in the middle of the small, one-room cabin, Tessa fought off panic. There was nowhere to hide, nowhere to escape the impending doom. She would be at Aaron's mercy. She heard voices outside the door. Aaron's and the guard's. A jolt of revulsion blasted through her like a bolt of lightning. The voices went silent.

What was going on? Had Aaron decided to leave her alone? *Oh, please, Lord, let it be.*

The doorknob turned.

Terror clawed through her.

Aaron swung the door open and stepped inside. "Honey, I'm home."

Tessa backed away until she bumped up against the dresser.

In long, purposeful strides, Aaron stalked forward. "We're going to have some fun!"

He crowded her into the corner, his hot breath making her gag as he swooped in, trying to plant a kiss on her lips.

She jerked her head away. "No, please don't do this."

He laughed. "Pop says I can do with you as I want." His sweaty hands clutched at her, pulling at the hem of her oversize sweatshirt. His intent to abuse her left her no choice but to defend herself.

With her hand cupped around her weapon, she swung her arm in a tight curve, hoping to disable him enough so she could escape his grasp. The sharp tip of the scissors pierced through his skin and lodged near his collarbone. He blinked at her in disbelief, his hand reaching for the scissors. She darted for the door.

He let out an enraged bellow and stumbled forward, grabbing on to her arm. She twisted away and rammed her free elbow into his solar plexus. He bent slightly with a loud exhale but didn't loosen his hold. She stomped as hard as she could on his instep.

He howled, his grip slipping on her arm.

Wildly, she punched at him, her fist connecting with the head of the scissors, driving them deeper into his flesh. He went to his knees, cursing her. She kicked out, her foot connecting with his shoulder, sending him toppling sideways. He landed in a heap. Aaron lay still, his eyes closed, his face lax.

Her lungs seized. Had she killed him?

For a horrific moment the reality of what she'd done swamped her. Her stomach heaved. Her lungs contracted painfully, forcing what little oxygen she had out in a violent exhale. Everything tilted. Darkness crept in at the corners of her mind.

*Oh, no.* She couldn't pass out. She had to move, to find Jeff. Shaking her head to clear her vision, she reached for the door as it burst open.

Jeff stood there with the guard's nasty-looking weapon in his hands, the barrel of the rifle pointed at her chest. His eyes widened, and he lowered the weapon.

A rush of emotion brought fresh tears to her eyes. He was alive and well. Her heart squeezed as affection and caring crowded out the horror of what she'd just done. She'd never been so happy to see anyone in her life. She rushed into his arms and hugged him tight. "Jeff."

He hugged her back for a split second, then set her away from him. His gaze bounced from her to Aaron on the floor, the blue tips of the shears sticking out of his body and blood pooling on the wooden floor.

"Whoa. Okay, then." Jeff looked at her with concern and approval. "You okay?"

She nodded, still clinging to him and barely daring to believe he was standing here. "How did you…?"

"I'll explain later." He released her and hurried to Aaron's still body, where he fished out a set of keys from the pocket of Aaron's khaki pants.

"Is he…dead?" she asked, her voice scarcely loud enough to be heard over the thundering of her heart. "We should check his pulse."

Jeff pressed two fingers to the uninjured side of Aaron's neck. "He has a pulse. Weak, but there."

She blew out a breath of relief.

Jeff grabbed her hand and yanked her out of the cabin. "Hurry. We don't have much time."

"But Aaron." She glanced back toward the

cabin with a wince as she stumbled after Jeff. "He could still die."

Jeff squeezed her hand. "It looks like you missed the artery. Someone will find him. Which means we need to be long gone by then."

She didn't know if she'd ever forget the sight of the scissors sticking out of the dip in Aaron's collar or the bright red blood. She glanced down at herself. Deep crimson splashes had soaked into her shirt, her sweatpants. She gagged.

She wished she could rewind the clock and go back to the moment of arriving at Glen Lake. She'd give anything for the only threat she faced to be a bacterium in the water. She'd rather be dissecting fish than be here running for her life.

The past seventy-two hours she'd been shot at, chased, made a prisoner, escaped, kissed and defended herself with a potentially deadly blow. This kind of stuff only happened in movies or books, not real life. Not her life. She longed for her lab, her petri dishes and microscopes.

Jeff tugged her toward the shed.

Confusion pulled her out of the quagmire of her thoughts. "Where are we going?

Instead of entering the shed, he led her behind the structure, where Ranger Randy was slumped against the wall.

Her heart leaped with joy and relief. "You're alive," she whispered, afraid he was only a vision her tormented mind had conjured up to block out what she'd done.

Randy gave her a weak smile. "Seems that way."

She flung her arms around him and hugged him.

The jingling of keys forced Tessa to release her hold on Randy.

"One of these has to be for the van," Jeff said.

She looked toward where the van sat only twenty yards away on the side of the warehouse. The other two trucks she'd seen earlier were gone.

"The minute you fire up the engine, the whole compound will come pouring out, and you'll never get away," Randy said. "Besides, there are other vehicles scattered about. They'll only chase you down."

"We have to try," Tessa said. "We can't go through the woods. You'd never make it."

"Don't worry about me," Randy said. "Save yourselves."

"We're taking the van and you," Jeff said, his voice hard and adamant. "What we need is a diversion."

"The generator," Randy said, pointing to the large contraption that powered the whole compound. "It's gas-powered."

"Good thinking," Jeff said. "An explosion would do the trick."

"But how? We don't have anything to ignite the gas with," Tessa asked. "A bullet won't do it."

She'd seen a TV show where they had debunked the idea that a single gunshot fired into a gas tank would make the tank explode. Only after multiple shots were fired was there an explosion and then only because the friction caused by the barrage of bullets had ignited the gasoline.

They didn't have that kind of time to experiment with the one rifle Jeff carried.

"I have something," Randy said. From his shirt pocket, he brought out a pack of cigarettes and a book of matches. "Mom always said these things would kill me. Guess she was right."

The horror of what he inferred flooded her veins. He intended to strike a match and toss it into the tank of gasoline, which meant he'd take the brunt of the blast. "No! You can't. You're coming with us."

Randy shook his head. "My life is over whether I go or stay. I'm either dead at my uncle's hand, or I'm toast in prison." He shrugged with a pessimistic certainty that grated on her already tightly strung nerves. "I'd rather be a hero and let you escape."

Tears burned her eyes. She gripped Jeff's arm. "You can't let him do this."

The grim expression on Jeff's handsome face and the sadness in his eyes tore at her heart. "My priority is you," he said softly. "I have to get you to safety."

Randy grabbed her hand. "It's okay. Please, go. Let me do this to make up for what my family has done."

Tears streamed in earnest down her face. How could she let him give up his life for them? "No. I won't allow it. We take our chances."

Randy released his hold on her and turned his gaze to Jeff. "Can you get me to the generator?"

She whirled on Jeff. "Don't you dare."

He placed his hands on her shoulders and stared deep into her eyes as he pressed the keys he'd taken from Aaron into her hand. "Go to the van and wait for me."

"No."

"Tessa, I know this is hard. But we have no choice. Let him do this."

Her heart in her throat, she closed her hand over the keys. "There has to be another way."

With regret deepening the blue of his handsome eyes, he shook his head. "Go. Now."

He gave her a little push, sending her stumbling toward the van. Her feet heavy, as if made of cement, she crossed the compound, sure that any second she'd be spotted and mowed down by a bullet.

It took every ounce of courage she had to put one foot in front of the other. She reached the van. Tears blurred her vision as she fumbled with the keys. Finally, she found the right one that slid into the lock to unlock the passenger-side door. She climbed inside and twisted in the seat to look out the back window of the van. Jeff and Randy were almost at the generator.

Her gaze fell to her duffel bag lying on the floor in the cargo hold. Adrenaline pumped through her veins.

She scrambled into the back, yanked open the zipper on the duffel and grabbed the flare gun. They could use it to start the fire that would explode the generator's gas tank. She opened the back of the van and ran, not caring how exposed she was. She couldn't let Randy kill himself for her.

Jeff grabbed her as she skidded to a stop by the generator. He yanked her to his chest. "What are you doing?"

"The flare gun," she panted, holding up her prize.

For a fraction of a second Jeff stared at the gun. Then he took it from her. "Okay, change of plans. The flare will ignite the gasoline."

Randy sat on the ground next to the generator's gas tank. He had the book of matches out and ready. The cap was off the tank and gasoline fumes filled the air, stinging Tessa's eyes. Randy held out his hand for the flare gun.

"Tessa, help Randy to the van," Jeff instructed.

"No, man, let me do this," Randy protested.

Her stomach twisted with renewed horror. She didn't want to leave Jeff behind. "What are you going to do?"

He gave her a breathtaking grin. "Blow something up!"

Concern and caring tore through her, leaving a raw trail in their wake.

Trusting Jeff to accomplish the task without getting himself killed prompted Tessa to send up another prayer. *God, I have to believe You'll see us through this.* They were still alive and fighting to stay that way.

Jeff's words echoed in her head: *God expects me to do all I can and trust the rest to Him.*

That was what they were doing. All they could and trusting the rest to God.

"Get to the van and be ready." He slid the rifle strap over Randy's head and settled it across his body. Then Jeff ripped the sleeve off his shirt and stuffed one end into the gas tank. Within seconds the soaked material dripped gasoline onto the ground. "I'll be coming in hot, so have the door open and the key in the ignition."

Urgency had her hauling Randy to his feet.

"Guess he gets to be the hero," Randy muttered with a crooked twist of his lips. "Thanks, Dr. Cleary."

She ignored the subtle sarcasm and took his words at face value. "You're welcome. Let's move."

They hurried as fast as Randy could hop on one foot to the van. Each step brought a wince of pain, twisting his face. Tessa couldn't let herself react to his injury. They had to get out of sight and be ready.

The door to the warehouse opened. Kyle stepped out. Tessa met the young man's gaze and silently pleaded with him not to give them away. His eyes widened, then he backed inside and shut the door.

The slight reprieve did nothing to ease her tension. She pushed Randy inside the back bed of the van, then she climbed into the passenger seat and stuck the key into the ignition before popping open the driver's-side door.

She watched through the back window. Jeff stood a few feet away from the generator and aimed the flare gun at the puddle of gas on the ground. Her heart slammed into her throat. The bright flash of the flare seized her breath. The gasoline caught fire.

"Hurry, hurry," she urged beneath her breath.

Jeff ran toward the van. Not daring to breathe, she prayed he made it to the van when the generator blew.

The tank exploded. The blast rocked the van just as Jeff jumped inside and cranked on the engine. He stepped on the gas, and the van shot forward. Within seconds, bullets riddled the back of the van as armed men dashed out of the buildings.

"Stay down," Jeff yelled.

Tessa scooted down but clamped a hand on Jeff's arm as if holding on to him would somehow protect him.

The van roared down the dirt road carved through the trees.

\* \* \*

Jeff drove the unfamiliar path, keeping half his attention on the rearview mirror. He hadn't had time to disable the truck he'd glimpsed behind the generator seconds before he fired the flare, successfully hitting the pool of gasoline leaking onto the ground.

He hadn't wanted to leave Tessa at risk one second longer than he absolutely had to. He'd let the danger get too close to her already. He wouldn't fail her again. He had to get her to safety.

Every second counted, and he had no illusions that a truck full of gun-toting men would not be hot on their tail before long. He kept the gas pedal floored.

"Everyone okay?" he asked, sending a worried glance toward Tessa, who sat hunched on the passenger seat looking as if she might throw up any second. Her complexion had a greenish hue beneath the pallor and her right hand gripped the door handle so hard, her knuckles had turned white.

He was so thankful she was alive, unharmed. When he'd heard Aaron's roar and then a scream, Jeff had imagined the worst.

But she'd taken Aaron down. Jeff couldn't be more proud of her.

And when she'd come running back from the van, he'd wanted to howl with rage at her, but then she'd handed him the flare gun and he'd realized, not for the first time, what a remarkable woman Dr. Tessa Cleary was.

Loyal, smart and brave. Affection and something else, something he wasn't ready to put a name to, bloomed in his heart. He knew emotions ran high during intense situations like this. What he was feeling would cool and go away once they were safe.

Then his focus would go back to where it belonged. Protecting the country and putting bad people behind bars.

And Tessa would resume her life without him.

That the thought left him hollow inside was an annoyance he didn't have time to examine.

The sight of the truck barreling down on them forced his attention away from the woman who was quickly charging around the walls he'd built to protect his heart.

"We've got company," Randy said from

the back. He'd propped himself up on Tessa's duffel bag.

"Yep. This thing won't go any faster," Jeff said.

"I'll try to buy us some time." Randy scooted toward the back doors.

Jeff glanced back and met Randy's gaze. "Make every bullet count."

"Check the glove box." Randy checked the ammo supply. "Knowing Aaron, there's got to be a handgun in there."

Without a word, Tessa opened the glove box. Sure enough, there was a Glock 9mm inside.

Jeff did a mental fist pump. "Okay. Tessa, I need you to trade places with me."

"What?" she squawked.

"Unless you think you can take them out with that gun?"

She shook her head. "How do we do this?"

"Slide over here." He waved her over. "Put your foot on the gas next to mine."

She did as he instructed.

"Take over the steering wheel." He made room for her hands as she squeezed over him until she was jammed up against the door.

He inhaled deeply of her scent; despite the ordeal and the grueling days, she smelled faintly of pine and still very feminine.

He scooted away from her as she took over driving. Once he was fully in the passenger seat, he checked the Glock, confirming it was loaded and ready. "Okay, Randy. Let's slow them down."

Randy popped open the back door and fired at the truck. Jeff rolled down the side window and wiggled out enough for a clear shot. He aimed for the front tires and pulled the trigger at the exact moment the van hit a rut. His bullet slammed into the other vehicle's grill.

A barrage of gunfire hit the van.

Randy slammed the door shut.

Jeff ducked back inside the cab. The sound of a tire exploding reverberated through the interior and set Jeff's teeth on edge. Tessa yelped as the van fishtailed, then shuddered to a limp.

"What do I do?" Tessa yelled, her voice surprisingly calm. No shrieking, no hysterics. He appreciated she wasn't freaking out.

"Keep your foot on the gas." The last thing they needed was to stop and be captured again.

Over the sound of the van struggling on the dirt road and the roar of the truck behind them, the distinct *whomp-whomp* of a helicopter sent Jeff's spirits bounding up with hope. He craned his neck to look up at the sky.

The camouflage netting Sherman used to hide his operation stretched above them, concealing the road. Irritated by the sight, Jeff leaned out the window and fired again at the truck, praying the good guys overhead would hear the sound and investigate. Doubtful, but one could hope.

"Jeff!" Tessa's shout brought his focus to the highway in front of them. She spun the steering wheel and the van skidded onto a blacktop road.

Jeff checked above them and was gratified to see that the netting ended at the tree line exactly where the truck chasing them stopped, then backed up out of sight.

Tossing the Glock onto the floor, Jeff climbed half out the passenger window to wave his arms, hoping to gain the attention of the people in the helicopter. It worked.

The helicopter circled and then slowly descended and set on the wide highway, the rotating blades stirring up the debris from the forest floor.

As soon as the van lurched to a stop, Jeff scrambled out. He met Tessa at the back doors. The relief on her face warmed his heart. He grabbed her and kissed her, the delightful sensation of her lush lips crushed against his eased the anxiety flowing through his system.

"Hey!" Randy inserted himself between them.

With a laugh, Jeff stepped back and helped Randy from the cargo hold. Tessa grabbed her duffel bag and then, with Randy propped between them, they ran for the waiting helicopter.

Once inside, Jeff shook hands with the special agent in charge, Doug Coleman.

"Where'd you come from?" Coleman shouted, trying to be heard over the rotors. "We've been searching these woods for the past two days."

Knowing there was too much to say, Jeff clapped Coleman on the back. "I'll give you a full report once we've set down."

Impatience flashed in Coleman's brown eyes, but he nodded and sat back. Jeff followed Coleman's curious gaze to Tessa. She sat next to Randy, fussing over the wound in his leg. Jeff imagined what his life was going to be like without her in it.

*Cold* and *lonely* were the words that came to mind. A state of being he should be used to. But until he'd met Tessa, he'd never experienced the level or depth of emotion for anyone that he had for her.

And that reality scared him no end. She'd made it clear her priority would always be her work. She'd walked away from one relationship already, choosing her career over love.

Jeff would never take the risk that Tessa would do the same to him if he was to admit how deeply entrenched she'd become in his heart over the past few days. The best thing for them both would be to get their lives back to normal.

Tessa's gaze met his, and she smiled, her

eyes full of tenderness. Separating would be the best thing all around. But it would also be the hardest thing he'd ever done.

# TEN

The command center teemed with men and women in flak vests, each with a different agency acronym emblazoned across the front. Feeling out of place, Tessa stood to the side of the room watching the melee of uniformed personnel who had taken over the visitors' center.

The helicopter that had picked them up on the lonely stretch of Highway 20 had set down in the town of Newhalem. The small Washington hamlet, owned by Seattle City of Lights, was the home base of the Skagit River Hydroelectric Project, and the company employed most of the town's inhabitants.

The local county sheriff, whom Tessa had met upon arriving at Glen Lake, joined Jeff and the men and women of the U.S. Border

Patrol, Homeland Security and the DEA as they gathered around a large map of the North Cascades National Forest. They were hoping to pinpoint the area where Sherman had his base of operation.

Apparently, this was where Jeff had disappeared to upon arriving, while she'd been given a change of clothes and ushered to one of the outer buildings, where she was able to freshen up. She couldn't wait to get to the hotel room they'd promised her so she could completely wash away the filth and grime from the ordeal in the woods. But that would have to wait. The first priority was raiding Sherman's compound before he got away.

Ranger Randy had been whisked off by a medic under heavy guard to another building to await transport to Bellingham, the nearest large town with a hospital.

She was so thankful he was going to live. Having his death on her conscience would have been too much. She was struggling enough with what she'd done to Aaron.

As she'd told the agents when she gave her statement, she still didn't know if he'd lived or died. She prayed he lived and was apprehended.

"This is approximately where we entered the forest." Jeff had one fist propped on the table while he pointed to a spot on the map. "We traveled by foot for seven hours before making camp. I believe we were headed in a northwest trajectory." He glanced over his shoulder. "What do you think, Tessa?"

Glad to be included, she stepped to his side. The affection in his eyes made her tongue stick to the roof of her mouth. She forced herself to say, "Yes. That's correct. But then we were driven to the compound. I had no sense of how long it took."

Jeff nodded in understanding. "Right. We had bags over our heads. Sherman's compound is roughly ten minutes by car from where they captured us in the forest."

"We scoured this whole area by air," the man Jeff had called Coleman said with a frown as he stared at the map. "The forest was too dense to see anything on the ground, and the thermal imaging kept recording messed-up data that made no sense."

"It's there," Jeff said. "They had camouflage netting strung up. Aaron, the second in command and Sherman's son, alluded to evasive tactics to keep infrared and thermal imaging from showing up. We blew their generator. You should have seen that despite the netting."

Coleman nodded. "We heard the explosion. Saw some smoke. That was what brought us back around to the area where we found you." He leaned forward and tapped the map. "Which was here." He spread his hand on the map. "This whole area needs to be thoroughly searched by ground." His gaze rested on Jeff, then Tessa. "Are there booby traps or deterrent devices we should know about?"

"I don't know." Jeff glanced at Tessa.

"What about Randy?" Anxiety kicked up its heels in her gut. She didn't want Jeff going back in. Nor did she want anyone else getting hurt. "He'd be able to tell you how to navigate anything deadly."

Coleman's gaze hardened. "Randy is refusing to give up any intel on his family or the illegal marijuana operation you found."

Frustrated by that surprising news, Tessa said, "Let me talk to him."

Jeff's hand came to rest on the small of her back. "It's worth a shot."

His support meant the world to her. He believed in her, in her abilities. No one had ever had her back before. Not like this. Not like Jeff had had her back over the past few days. She couldn't have made it without him.

He'd saved her time and time again. But more than what he'd done to keep her physically safe, he'd made her believe in herself, believe that she was strong enough to fight for her life. She would be eternally grateful to him.

She forced her mind to the moment at hand. Mr. Coleman stared at her as if waiting for an answer to a question she hadn't heard. "I'm sorry, can you repeat that?"

"You okay?" The concern in Jeff's voice sent a ribbon of warmth winding around her. He tugged her closer.

She drew herself up. "Yes. Tired. But I'm good." She turned back to Coleman. "Sir, you asked a question?"

Coleman's intense gaze pinned her to the spot. "Do you really think he'll talk to you?"

"He'd been willing to give up his life for

us," she said. A fact she still had trouble wrapping her mind around. But she'd found a way to keep Randy from sacrificing himself and they were all able to escape. "I feel confident he'll tell me what you need to know."

Coleman considered her a moment, then slowly inclined his head. "Agent Steele, you good to accompany Dr. Cleary?"

"Yes, sir. Glad to."

Jeff propelled her out of the visitor center, a decidedly newer structure than the rest of Newhalem. The small company town consisted of a handful of buildings dating back to the early 1900s, some showing signs of renovations. "Are you really okay?"

She tucked her arm through his, her gaze on the old Baldwin steam locomotive engine not far away. The black beast gleamed in the late-afternoon sun. "I am now that we're away from the woods and that awful place."

"Soon you'll be in a hotel with room service," he said.

"And a hot bath." Muscles she didn't even know she had ached. Her skin was raw and scraped. Her nails were jagged and grimy. As much as she loved the outdoors and relished her time in the field, she would be happy to get back to her lab and her tests and her computer.

They walked across the dirt street running the length of the town. A dog's bark snagged her gaze. She caught a glimpse of an older man walking a black dog on a leash as they turned the corner of a building and disappeared. Her steps faltered. Her skin prickled. She knew him.

"Something wrong?" Jeff took her hand.

"I don't think so." At least she hoped not. "I thought I saw someone I recognized."

"Who?

"Henry. I never got his last name. He was at the ranger station when I arrived at Glen Lake. He had the same kind of dog, too."

"I remember him. Kind of a crotchety old man."

"That's the one." Why would Henry be here in Newhalem?

"Stay right here," Jeff said and took off at a jog for the place where she'd seen the older man and dog go. Jeff disappeared around the corner and returned a moment later. He shook his head as he came back to her. "No one there."

She shrugged. "I must be more tired than I thought. It couldn't have been Henry."

They proceeded to a historic building that looked in need of some rehabilitation. A sign over the doorway read Gorge Inn. A uniformed sheriff's deputy stood watch at the entrance. Inside the main room of the rustic structure, a bed had been set up with an IV connected to Randy's arm while he awaited transportation to the hospital in Bellingham.

He lay stretched out on a metal-frame bed. His eyes were closed, his face pale. The bandage around his leg had been changed for a pristine white one. Thankfully, they'd managed to get the bleeding to stop. The town's physician had said Randy was stable but would need surgery.

She approached the side of the bed. Jeff grabbed a ladder-back chair and brought it over for her. She sat and took Randy's cold hand in hers.

His eyelids fluttered open and focused on her. He gave her a crooked smile. "I didn't think I'd see you again."

Her heart twisted. If only she'd come to check on him, to wish him a speedy recovery and thank him again for helping her break Jeff out and leading them both away from his uncle's camp. But no. They had come to his bedside to ask him to betray his kin once more. "We need your help."

His gaze slid away. "I've done what I could."

She squeezed his hand, drawing his attention back to her. "You did a great thing by helping us escape, Randy. I have to believe you aided us because you know what your uncle and cousin are doing in those woods is wrong. You said yourself, the men there are trapped, held prisoner. No one should be held captive and enslaved, forced to work under the threat of bodily harm."

Randy heaved a sigh. "It wasn't supposed to be like that. The compound was supposed to be a refuge for those without hope and nowhere else to turn. But after Aunt Katherine's death, Uncle Sherman changed, became bitter and mean and greedy. Then when he had the car accident that left him crippled and killed his daughter, Sarah, he refused to allow anyone to leave the compound. He sold the plants for profit. He listened to Aaron. My cousin has always had a chip on his shoulder. For as long as I can remember, he felt like the world owed him something. His mom and his sister died. His dad was a cripple. He didn't think it was fair."

"Life isn't always fair," she said, recalling the many times her grandmother had said the same thing whenever she bemoaned the state of her life or a situation she didn't like. Now Grandma's words resonated deeply within her. "God never promised that."

Randy's lips twisted. "Aaron doesn't believe in God. He doesn't believe in much of anything."

Her heart contracted in her chest. "Randy, there's something you should know." Her throat threatened to close on the words but she had to get them out. "I injured Aaron trying to get away from him."

He blinked, his eyes growing round. "Did he hurt you?"

Touched that his first thought was for her, she shook her head. "No. But he would have."

"Yes, he would have." Randy looked away. "He hurt a lot of people."

"Which is why the police need to go in and free those men," she said. "They need to know where the cameras and motion detectors are located. And if there is any type of trap or anything else that would prevent them from entering the compound."

At his hesitation, she pressed, "Randy, you're our only hope of getting those men out alive. You've come this far. You need to think of yourself now. If you help the authorities, they may be more lenient with you."

"My family is never going to speak to me again," he said quietly. "They'll blame me for all the trouble."

She didn't know what to say to that.

Jeff stepped closer, placing a hand on her shoulder. "Doing the right thing is sometimes difficult. But you have to be able to live with yourself in the end. Your decision could save lives or take lives. What kind of man do you want to be?"

Randy swallowed. "I'll tell you what I can."

"Thank you." Tessa leaned in to place a

kiss on the younger man's cheek. "You're making the right decision."

"I'll have an agent come take your statement," Jeff said. "I'll put in a good word with the state's attorney."

"I'd appreciate it," Randy said and closed his eyes.

Jeff led Tessa from the building. "You handled him well."

Pleased he thought so, she said, "Thank you. I like Randy. I think he's been caught between his family loyalty and his conscience."

"Well, good for us that his conscience is winning out," Jeff said, steering her back to the visitors' center. Once there, Jeff reported to Coleman and then made arrangements for Tessa to be transported to Bellingham, where she would take a plane back to Utah in the morning.

"You're not coming with me?" she asked as he walked her to the waiting SUV.

"No. I want to be in on the raid of Sherman's compound."

She stopped by the back end of the vehicle. "Why? Haven't you had enough of that place?"

"Yes, actually. But I want to make sure Sherman is taken into custody. I don't want there to be any mistakes made. The man alluded to friends in high places as being part of why he could operate undetected for so long. I want to make sure he doesn't get away with his crimes."

"For a man who professes to not do commitment, you're very committed to your job."

"Those are two very different types of commitment you're talking about," he said, his expression wary.

"Maybe, but both require attention, patience, dedication. There's a risk with both, as well," she said, realizing that her words were just as true for herself as for him. "You could lose your job and have nothing to show for the commitment you gave it."

His gaze narrowed. "That's true. But a job won't leave a heart in tatters."

His words brought her up short. "Who was she?"

"No one."

"Is she still in your life?"

"No!"

So that was why he was afraid to commit to

a relationship. A woman broke his heart. The thought reverberated through her mind and resonated deep within her own heart. Who was she to judge him when she, too, had the same fear? "Then why are you still letting her affect how you live and what you do?"

Another question she had to ask herself regarding Michael. Funny how it was so easy to see other people's issues clearly and not recognize them in oneself.

He stiffened. "Don't try to analyze me, please."

A wry smile escaped. She was as loath to reveal her inner turmoil as he was. "I might not like what I find?"

"Something like that." He cupped her cheek, the pad of his thumb rubbing across her bottom lip. "I'm going to miss you."

Her heart fluttered, and emotions bubbled up from the depths of her heart, making her want to throw her arms around his waist and cling to him. Staring into his eyes, she sifted through the complex emotions burrowing into her heart and soul. She was profoundly grateful to him for so many reasons—not only had he protected her, making sure she left the woods alive and unharmed, he'd made her feel special and cared for.

Not once had he found fault with her; not once had he patronized or degraded her thoughts, opinions or actions. Sure, there were moments when they had not agreed, like when he told her he was coming along in the boat, but never once had he been disrespectful.

Over the course of the past few days, she'd grown to care for him in a way she'd never cared for anyone else. She admired his strength of character, his integrity and commitment to justice, to his faith, to her. He may not want to give his heart away, but Jeff Steele was a man worthy of trust. A man to count on, whether times were hard or easy.

There was a bond between them that could only come from having survived an ordeal like they had. She told herself the emotions crowding her chest stemmed from the intensity of the situation, from facing horror and death. That once she was back home, her feelings would fade and in time all this would be a memory to pull out occasionally.

However, her mind, her heart, refuted that

notion with a sardonic laugh that rang in her ears, mocking her attempt to deny that she'd fallen in love with this man.

Her breath stalled. She had fallen in love with Jeff.

Words rose, bittersweet on the back of her tongue. She held them in. He'd made it clear a relationship wasn't what he wanted. She wasn't even sure if she did. They barely knew each other, yet she felt as if they'd spent a lifetime together. But complicating the situation with words and emotions that would lead only to a broken heart wasn't something she could bring herself to do. Instead, she entwined her arms around his neck and drew him closer, putting all the love and affection and caring and respect and honor she could into a kiss.

His arms snaked around her, tugging her close until their bodies were flush, their hearts beating in time together. She never wanted this moment to end. He withdrew his lips from hers. A whimper of loss escaped from her throat. He dropped his forehead to hers.

"I'm really going to miss you," he repeated, his voice husky and low.

She forced a brave smile. "I'll miss you, too."

For several heartbeats they stayed connected. The world around them seemed to have faded. The beauty of the surrounding mountains, the sweet scent of pine in the air, converged into nothingness.

All that mattered were these last few moments together. Moments she wanted to engrave on her heart for all time.

Her pulse spiked as if she'd run a mile. Suddenly, the future loomed bleak and unwelcoming without him in it. Unwilling to let him go, she said, "You could come visit me. Utah's not that far from Washington. No strings attached. Just friends."

He lifted his head, his eyes tender. "It would be better for us both if I don't."

She swallowed back a protest. Maybe better for him. He was done with the moment, with her. She shouldn't be hurt. He'd never made a promise or overture that could lead her to believe he felt the same. "I understand."

He stepped back and opened the SUV's door. "Agent Tremont will take you to Bellingham."

The man sitting behind the wheel saluted

her. The corners of her mouth lifted in what she hoped resembled a smile, but feared looked more like a grimace.

"You'll stay there tonight and be on the first flight out in the morning."

She didn't trust herself to speak. She could only nod.

"Thank you, Tessa."

Tilting her head, she managed to ask, "For?"

"You said you'd find the source of the contamination and put a stop to it. And you did."

She'd been so naive and arrogant that first day when she'd arrived at Glen Lake. The "expert" come to save the fish and protect those who used the lake. She'd thought she could fix everything alone. She'd thought she didn't need anyone, not her team from the Fish and Aquatic Ecology Unit, not God. And certainly not Jeff.

But she did need him, her heart cried out.

Sadness descended, upping her fatigue and tension.

"We did it together. As a team," she reminded him and placed her hand over his heart. "You're a good man, Agent Jeff Steele. Our country is a safer place because of you."

"Not yet. Once we have Sherman in custody and dismantle his operation, then our country and our neighbors to the north will be safer."

"Be careful, please." Renewed worry camped out in her chest.

"I will." He captured her hand. "Goodbye, Tessa."

Slipping her hand away, she squared her shoulders and pushed her emotions down as far as they'd go inside her soul. She climbed into the SUV. He shut the door with a final click. A moment later, the vehicle rolled away.

Twisting in the seat, she took one last look at Jeff, his dark hair gleaming in the autumn sun. "Goodbye, my love," she whispered, resigning herself to never seeing him again.

She was alone once more.

*God will not abandon us.*

Clinging to Jeff's words and to the faith he'd helped her to renew, she sent up a prayer. "Keep him safe, Lord."

# ELEVEN

Jeff watched the SUV until it disappeared from view. He rubbed at the hollow spot in his chest where his heart had caved in on itself. Letting her go was excruciatingly painful, like nothing he'd ever endured. But it was the right thing to do. For both their sakes. She was a bright and shining moment during a dark and nasty ordeal. He'd come to care deeply for her, but she had a full life that had no room for him.

He wasn't good at relationships. He wasn't good at committing. Despite how independent and self-reliant Tessa appeared, she was a woman who longed for commitment. But committing meant letting his heart get attached. Attachment made him vulnerable to the hurt that would eventually come as it always did when he let himself get too close to anyone. Growing up he'd loved every nanny who'd come to stay, and his heart had died a little when each one left.

Then he'd met Janie. For a brief time he'd thought she'd healed his heart, but in the end, she'd left him, too.

He couldn't take that kind of heartache again.

A mocking voice inside his head chimed in, *What makes you think you aren't already attached to Tessa?*

He blew out a breath. Okay, maybe he was a little attached to Tessa. They'd just survived a horrendous ordeal together. They'd bonded in many ways, but that didn't change the fact that their futures were on different paths.

And if he kept reminding himself of that, eventually he'd come to peace with living without her.

Resolving not to think about her or the emptiness inside his heart, he returned to the visitors' center, where the tactical team prepared for the assault on the compound.

He was handed an assault rifle and a Kevlar vest.

"We're good to go," Coleman said.

Jeff checked the clip on the rifle and then put on the vest as anticipation revved in his blood. They piled inside a convoy of SUVs. Randy had explained about the motion detectors set along the side of the highway set to send a warning to Sherman when anyone came off the main road and took the dirt road carved through the trees.

When the convoy reached the dirt road, they found the wiring for the motion detectors and looped the circuit, making the way passable without detection.

A half mile away from the compound, the convoy stopped, and the teams piled out. They would go the rest of the way on foot.

"Stay alert," Coleman said in a hushed voice. "They are heavily armed."

Jeff led the way as the men spread out and worked a path through the trees. The smoke from the generator explosion had long evaporated, but the smell of burning gasoline lingered in the air. When they reached the compound, the place looked deserted. Not a man in sight. And thankfully, no dogs.

Keen to arrest Sherman, Jeff motioned to

Coleman that he was taking the house. Coleman nodded. Jeff peeled off and hustled for the house, his assault weapon up, his gaze watchful for signs of movement. Two tact team members followed him. Jeff was glad for the backup.

He reached the porch and flattened himself near the front window. An eerie sensation made his fingers tighten around the rifle. Why had Sherman let him get this close? The man had to know they were here.

Jeff peered through the break in the curtains. The house appeared empty, too. No movement. No signs of life inside. He moved so he could look through the window at a different angle. A chair had been positioned in the entryway. He had a bad feeling this was a trap.

He motioned for the men to fall back. Using the butt of the rifle, he broke out the front window. Before climbing inside, he checked the floor for trip wires and found a thin cord leading to the chair. Jeff stepped over the wire with one foot and froze balanced half in, half out of the window as his gaze landed on the seat of the chair facing the front door. The seat was filled with C-4.

Another cord attached to a pin in the explosive led to the door handle. Whoever opened the door would be blown to smithereens along with anyone in close proximity.

Heart hammering, he backed out of the window. Coleman joined him on the porch.

"It's a booby trap," Jeff said. "The house is rigged to explode."

Coleman's nostrils flared. He motioned with his hands and yelled, "Fall back. Explosives!"

Once they were a safe distance away, Coleman requested a bomb squad to join them at the compound.

"We cleared the buildings." Coleman gestured toward the compound at large. "We didn't come across anyone matching the description of Sherman or Aaron. But you should take a look to be sure they aren't hiding in plain sight."

The tactical team had rounded up the men working the illegal marijuana operation and had them corralled, sitting in a tight circle in the center of the compound.

A glance was all Jeff needed. "No, they aren't here." He searched for Emil among the men. "Neither are any of the men who'd been part of the security force."

Jeff's gaze landed on Kyle, the young man who'd brought them food when he and Tessa were first brought to the compound.

Grabbing Kyle by the collar, Jeff dragged him to his feet. "Where are Sherman and all the guards?"

Kyle shrank back. "I don't know. After the explosion, they took off."

"Where to?" Jeff shook him.

"I don't know," the younger man said. "They left as fast as they could."

Jeff released him. Kyle sank back to the ground, drawing his knees to his chest, making him look more like the teenager he was than a hardened criminal.

Swiping a hand through his hair, Jeff fought to control the frustration coursing through his veins. He would track Sherman down to the ends of the earth if need be. "Did you find Aaron's body?"

"No bodies," Coleman said.

"Did Sherman bury Aaron?" Jeff asked the group of men.

"He's not dead," one man offered.

"So Aaron lived." Jeff gritted his teeth, conflicted by the information. On one hand it was good news for Tessa's sake. She hadn't taken another person's life. She didn't deserve that burden. On the other hand, Aaron would be even more dangerous wounded and angry. "He would need a hospital."

Coleman nodded. "I'll send out an alert to all medical facilities within a two-hundred-mile radius. They couldn't have gone farther than that yet."

"Unless they flew," Jeff pointed out.

Turning to the group of men with their downcast eyes and bowed shoulders, his empathy tugged at him. Randy had said most of these men were homeless or runaways who'd been promised a better life only to end up enslaved, working for long hours and kept high on drugs as a means of controlling them. "Does anyone here know where Sherman and Aaron were headed?"

Kyle's chin lifted. "Aaron kept yelling stuff

about getting even with the lady who stuck him with the scissors."

Jeff's stomach twisted with dread. Would Aaron make good on his threat to exact revenge on Tessa? Fear rippled through him.

"We have to secure Dr. Cleary," Jeff told Coleman. "She's not safe until Aaron Roscha and his father, Sherman, are apprehended."

Coleman used a satellite phone to call the agent who'd escorted Tessa to Bellingham. "Agent Tremont, where is Dr. Cleary?"

As Coleman listened to the answer, Jeff curled his fingers to prevent himself from ripping the phone out of Coleman's hand so he could hear what was happening. Anxiety twisted in his gut. He wanted to assure himself Tessa was safe.

"Keep a close eye on her. I'm sending more men to help protect her," Coleman instructed before hanging up. "She just checked into the hotel in Bellingham. Tremont will stand guard outside her door."

Tessa was still a target. She wouldn't be safe until Aaron and his father were behind bars. Jeff had to arrest Aaron and Sherman before they had a chance to hurt Tessa. He couldn't live if something happened to her.

Tessa changed into the new clothes she'd bought in the hotel's gift shop. Normally not one for sweat suits but growing fonder of them after this experience, she couldn't resist the bright lemon-colored fleece-lined two-piece set with the city's name emblazoned on the thigh of the pants and across the chest of the jacket. The T-shirt underneath had a silk-screened image of nearby Mount Baker.

As souvenirs went, the outfit would be a reminder of surviving her ordeal in the North Cascades Forest.

Her hair was damp from the bath and wildly out of control. She should have bought a hair tie to tame her curls, but it felt so good to be clean and warm, she supposed she could live with unruly. As she towel-dried her hair, she wandered over to the lone square window. The three-star hotel faced the airport. The roar of jets taking flight ricocheted off the walls of the room.

At least the place was dirt-free and she was

safe. Agent Tremont had said he'd be right outside if she needed anything.

How about Jeff's love?

Shaking her head at her own folly for falling in love with a man who didn't believe in commitment, she lay on the bed, relishing the cushioned softness. She'd never take a mattress for granted again. Part of her wanted to curl up and go to sleep, to find solace in her dreams rather than face the reality that she would never see Jeff again. Not that she thought sleep would come easily. Her emotions were too raw; her heart still beat too fast, and her stomach was tied in knots.

She should be elated to be returning to her own home and her work.

But returning to a lonely apartment, to a lonely office, to a lonely lab, didn't appeal anymore.

She'd always told herself she was better off without family. Her parents had their own lives, lives that didn't include her. She had no siblings, no cousins. No hope for a romance on the horizon. At least not with the man who'd captured her heart in the depths of an ancient forest.

Her gaze was drawn to the framed photograph hanging over the king-size bed. A majestic waterfall in black-and-white captured on print by a famous Pacific Northwest photographer should have been awe-inspiring. Instead, the image evoked all the terror she'd experienced from the last waterfall she'd seen.

To distract herself from her memories and her heartache, she grabbed the television remote. Maybe some mindless TV would help ease the chaos going on in her mind. She searched the channels, bypassing every sitcom and drama until she landed on the local news station, anxious for the commercials to end.

The local news should have a report on the illegal marijuana farm in the North Cascades Forest. The raid on Sherman's operation would be a big deal and newsworthy. Maybe she'd catch a glimpse of Jeff.

Her heart squeezed tight with hope and throbbed with sadness at the same time.

A thud outside the door jolted her attention from the television. Her heart grabbed her by the throat.

"Calm down," she groused to herself. "It's only Agent Tremont bumping the door." She stood and padded barefoot across the room. Despite what she told herself, she put the U-shaped security latch on and slowly opened the door enough to peer out. The hall was empty. "Agent Tremont?"

When he didn't respond, dread crept up her spine. Biting her lip, she debated stepping out into the hall to see if she could find Tremont. Deciding it would be better to call the front desk and have them send a security guard to check on the agent, she pushed the door closed, but before it could latch, something large and heavy rammed into it, sending the door flying inward, ripping the latch off the wall and propelling her backward. She landed on the floor with a painful thud.

A man stepped into the room and loomed over her.

Aaron.

She blinked, praying this was a nightmare, one she desperately wanted to wake up from. But the fear slithering through her was all too real. He held something black and sinister-looking in his hand. Panic quivered inside her. She scuttled backward, desperate to get away from him, but there was nowhere for her to go.

Aaron's flat, cold eyes stared at her, and his lips curled in a cruel smile. "Miss me?"

She screamed.

He leveled the weapon at her. A blinding light stunned her eyes for a second before something shot out from the end of the gun and found its mark in her stomach. Agonizing pain exploded within her as every muscle in her body stiffened. Shock waves pulsated through her body, causing her heart to pump erratically. A loud keening filled her head.

Regret for not telling Jeff she loved him swamped her. Tears burned her eyes. The world faded to a pinprick of light. The pain stopped. Her body went limp. A silent scream of protest echoed through her mind. Then the light went out.

Jeff stalked down the hall of the house tucked away in the woods in search of Sherman's office. He passed the room he'd once stayed in. He thought of the night Tessa had broken him out. She'd been so brave to risk her life for him when she could have escaped so much more easily without him. She and Randy could have slipped away unnoticed for hours. Jeff would have done all he could to buy them time to get as far away as possible. But instead, she'd freed him. It meant the world to him. She meant the world to him.

His heart ached with regret for what could never be. Once the danger to her was finally put to an end, she would go back to Utah and undoubtedly her memories of him would fade. Though he knew he would never forget her. There would always be a special spot in his heart for her.

In Sherman's office, Jeff yanked open the drawers of the desk. Nothing but the usual office stuff—paper clips, pens, stationery—empty files, receipts for supplies and food for the compound, but nothing to indicate where he and Aaron were headed.

Most of the documents in the file cabinets had been shredded. What little remained wasn't useful. And no computer, only the monitor left on the desk.

Jeff slammed a fist on the desktop. He stalked back to the living room.

Coleman walked out of the kitchen. "Come up with anything?"

"No. You?"

"Nada." Coleman moved to the front window, where Jeff had broken out the glass, and stared out at the men seated on the ground with their hands now tied behind their backs. "We'll take them all in and question them individually. One of them has to know something."

"That could be." But by the time each man was questioned, Sherman, Aaron and the other guards could be anywhere.

At least Tessa would be safe. Jeff would make sure someone watched over her every minute until Aaron was caught.

Coleman's satellite phone rang. He answered and stepped away.

Jeff needed to see Tessa, to tell her what was happening, to give her a heads-up that Aaron was still alive.

When Coleman hung up, he turned toward Jeff; the expression on the agent's face sent dread slicing through Jeff.

"The extra agents arrived at the hotel. They found Agent Tremont unconscious in the stairwell."

Fear ate a hole through Jeff's heart. "Tessa?"

"Gone."

The air left Jeff's lungs in a rush. He clenched his fists. He never should have left her side. Now they had her.

"The hotel's security video shows Aaron approaching her room. But the camera was then disabled."

Meaning they didn't know if Tessa was alive or dead.

Deep, aching sorrow filled him. No! He wouldn't believe the worst. She had to be still alive. But for how long?

Not willing to give up hope, Jeff said, "There has to be something here that tells us where Sherman would go."

"His private quarters?"

Nodding, Jeff turned and rushed to the wing Sherman occupied. Here, like the rest of the house, showed signs of a woman's touch. A beautifully carved four-poster bed in a rich cherrywood and a rose-patterned floral-print coverlet with frilly throw pillows dominated the master suite. Lace curtains and a rose-colored armchair sat by the window. A vanity set with a bottle of perfume and a silver hairbrush was tucked into the corner. Sherman apparently still clung to the memories of his wife and hadn't redecorated after her death.

Before meeting Tessa, Jeff wouldn't have understood such sentiment, nor would he have appreciated the sense of loss Sherman must have felt when his wife passed on.

But now, facing a life without Tessa in it, Jeff knew all too well the heartache of losing the love of his life.

Stunned by that revealing thought, he gripped the doorjamb as the world shifted. He loved Tessa.

He'd been trying to deny it, to push away the feelings crowding his chest, rationalizing that he was protecting himself by not admitting that he'd fallen deeply, madly in love with Tessa. But he had.

And now she was gone.

Rage nipped at him. Sherman, at least, had been able to say goodbye to his wife before she succumbed to the cancer that had claimed her life.

Jeff wanted a chance to tell Tessa how he felt and to see if they could make a future together. He wanted a lifetime with her. But first he had to figure out where Aaron had taken her.

He prayed he'd find her in time, before anything... No! He couldn't think that way. He had to stay focused and locate Sherman. He'd lead Jeff to Aaron and Tessa.

With determination, Jeff assessed the room with a more critical eye. The drawers to the matching dresser were open, clothes flung all over as if someone had quickly picked through them. He checked the contents of the drawers though he knew he wouldn't find anything.

Wheel tracks marred the plush carpet to the walk-in closet. Women's clothes took up one side of the closet, while empty hangers dangled on the other side. With a growl he flicked the empty hangers and set them swinging.

Desperation clawed at his throat. He could barely take a breath as he hurried from the house and rushed to the circle of men. "Listen to me. I need your help. Is there anything any of you know that could help us find Sherman and Aaron? It's a matter of life and death. They have Dr. Cleary. Where would they take her?"

No one spoke. Frustrated, Jeff squatted down in front of Kyle. "Any ideas?"

Kyle shook his head. "I don't know where he'd go. The only one who might is Randy."

"Coleman." Jeff straightened and turned to the agent. "Do you have a number for the Bellingham hospital?"

"Here." Coleman handed him his phone. "This is the number of the agent assigned to Randy's detail."

Jeff made the call, explained that he needed to talk to Randy, but he was told Randy was being prepped for surgery. Jeff's hand tightened on the phone. "As soon as he's out of surgery and conscious, I need to speak to him."

At a loss, he ran a hand through his hair. His mind scrambled to come up with a viable plan. Wait. If Randy was Sherman's nephew, then who were Randy's parents and where were they? And would they know where Sherman and Aaron would go?

"I need to use a computer," Jeff told Coleman.

"There's a laptop in the Suburban," he said. "Come on."

They hurried into the woods, where they'd left the SUVs. Jeff needed to search for the rest of Sherman Roscha's family. His only hope was that one of them would be able to help him locate Tessa. He had to find her. And when he did, he was never going to let her out of his sight again.

He sent up a silent plea. *Oh, Lord, please let Tessa be alive. Let me get to her before anything happens to her.*

Using Coleman's laptop, Jeff searched every database he could think of to learn more about Randy and Sherman and came up with some good information. But there was no sense of triumph, only a driving urgency to do what he could to save Tessa.

"Randy's mother is Sherman's sister," Jeff told Coleman. "Sherman also has another brother, named Henry Roscha. It has to be the same Henry Tessa saw in Newhalem right before she left for Bellingham. It couldn't be a coincidence that Henry owns a bait-and-tackle store at Glen Lake and is related to Sherman."

"Where does the sister live?"

"Seattle."

"We have a BOLO out at every airport. If

Sherman or his son, Aaron, show up at Sea-Tac, they'll be detained."

"He wouldn't be that stupid. If they intend to fly out of the country, they'd go to one of the private airstrips. Henry will know if his brother has a plane and where he keeps it. I need to go to Glen Lake," Jeff said.

"Agreed." Coleman handed him the keys to one of the Suburbans they'd arrived in. "Take a team with you. If you find out anything, let me know, okay?"

"Will do." Jeff took the keys Coleman dangled.

With two tactical team members joining him, Jeff sped to Glen Lake in a blaze of flashing lights and siren. He parked in front of the ranger station just as Ranger George stepped out to greet him.

"Agent Steele, we're so glad you're okay," George said offering his hand. "We joined the search party and looked for days before word came that you'd been found. How is Dr. Cleary?"

Jeff's stomach tightened. "Not good. Do you know where to find Henry Roscha?"

Surprise widened George's eyes. "Yeah,

sure. He owns a small store at the dock on the right side of the shore at the halfway mark of the lake. Most everyone in this area or those who use the lake shops at Henry's store. He carries lots more than just bait and tackle."

"Can you take me there?"

"I can. Why?"

Jeff wasn't sure what to make of the reluctant expression on the older ranger's face, nor was he sure how much to share. For all Jeff knew, the ranger could be part of Sherman's network. Or a relative, even. "I have some questions for him. Is there a problem?"

"Henry also breeds Rottweilers. Sometimes the dogs aren't too friendly."

Ah. That explained the reluctance. Jeff had been right. Sherman kept the dogs close by. That was how the canines had arrived so quickly to track them down when they'd escaped from the house. Jeff should have made the connection to the dog he'd seen with the old man at the ranger station. But Jeff had been a little preoccupied trying to keep Tessa alive.

Sherman must have called his brother, who had brought his animals to the compound to be used to find them in the woods. All they would have needed were the pillows from the beds Tessa or Jeff had slept on or the towels from the bathroom to give the dogs their scent.

"I'll take my chances," Jeff said. "I want to go to Henry's store and his house."

"Well, that will be easy enough," Ranger George said. "Henry built a cabin behind the store."

"Good. Take us there."

"Let me tell Jean." George ducked back inside the ranger station house that also doubled as a home for the ranger and his wife.

Anxious to find Henry Roscha and discover if he knew where his brother had run to, Jeff jumped behind the wheel and revved the engine.

George returned a few minutes later and climbed into the passenger seat of the SUV. The two tact members sat in the back, silent and intimidating.

A lanyard with a slew of keys hung around George's neck. Jeff eyed the many keys.

"I have keys to all the lake residences on this side of the border," George said.

Following the ranger's directions, Jeff arrived at the bait-and-tackle store near a dock on the east side of the lake. The store was closed up tight. Jeff went around back to the small, one-level house. An oversize enclosed pen contained five large Rottweilers.

As he approached, the dogs barked, the noise rising to deafening levels. Ignoring the animals, Jeff pounded on the door to Henry's home. No one answered. George picked through the keys on his lanyard until he found the one that fit into the lock on the door.

"I won't get in trouble for letting you in here, will I?" Harris asked.

"No. I have probable cause, considering Dr. Cleary has been kidnapped by Sherman and Aaron, known relatives of Henry's," Jeff explained. "If it will make you feel better, you can give me the keys and I'll go inside while you go back to the station."

"That won't be necessary." George unlocked the door and stepped aside to allow Jeff access.

Inside the cabin was dark. No sign of Henry. It appeared he'd skipped town along with his brother.

Jeff prayed with desperation that he would find a clue somewhere inside the home as to where Sherman and his family had fled to, because Jeff was quickly running out of ideas.

The longer Tessa was in Aaron's clutches, the closer she came to death.

If she wasn't already dead.

# TWELVE

The bright white light beckoned to Tessa. But why was she so cold? She must be somewhere between life and death. Part of her wanted to go be with God. There would be peace and comfort. Warmth. She would see her grandmother again.

But there was still so much she wanted to do before surrendering her earthly life. Going into the light would mean leaving Jeff behind forever.

She'd never have a chance to tell him how much she loved him and wanted a future with him. She'd never have a chance to convince him that somehow they could make a relationship work and that she was worth the risk of commitment.

She wanted to tell him she was willing to

risk giving her heart to him. That no matter how scary letting down her defenses was, life without Jeff terrified her worse than facing Aaron and his gun.

Sure, there were logistics to consider. It would make more sense for her to relocate to Blaine, since Jeff moving to Utah wouldn't be realistic—there was no international borderline to patrol.

And the Pacific Northwest had plenty of forests with lakes and streams for her to study.

"Wake up!" a deep voice demanded.

Tessa's eyes fluttered fully open. The bright white light came into focus as a bare halogen bulb hanging from a long cord attached to the steel rafters overhead. Alongside the bulb was Aaron's face.

Her nightmare hadn't ended. She wasn't dead. Deep talons of terror shredded through her, making her shrink back as awareness rushed in. She lay on a hard concrete floor. They were in a drafty metal building that smelled like automotive grease and gasoline.

"It's about time you came to," Aaron snarled.

She moved to sit up, but her body wouldn't

cooperate. Her muscles quivered with exhaustion as if she'd run twenty miles uphill. Ropes bit into her wrists and ankles. A burning sensation in her abdomen reminded her she'd been shot.

She jerked her gaze to her stomach, expecting to see gore and blood, but there was nothing marring the yellow jacket she'd bought at the hotel's gift shop.

Memories of that moment rushed in. She hadn't realized at first what Aaron held when he'd busted into her hotel room but as he'd fired, she'd seen the probes eject in a flurry of confetti. He'd shot her with a stun gun. A nonlethal way of incapacitating a person.

Relief sent another round of shaking through her muscles and she laid her head down on the bitter-cold concrete floor. Thankfully, she didn't have a bullet lodged in her stomach, but she wasn't sure she wanted to know why Aaron hadn't killed her. Whatever he had planned would probably make her long for death.

Averting her gaze from her enemy, she realized they were in a hangar. A sleek private jet with the strangest U-shaped tail she'd ever seen stood a few feet away. The plane's door was open and a ramp bridged the gap to the ground. Obviously Sherman was close by.

"Where are we?" Her voice came out rough and weak.

"The question is, where are we going?" Aaron laughed.

Biting back her frustration and fear, she finally struggled to a seated position. "Okay, where are we going?"

"Someplace nice." His grin held enough malice to curdle her stomach. "Though you won't be coming. We won't need you for much longer. Then I can kill you." He placed a hand over his collarbone, reminding her that she'd stabbed him with a pair of scissors.

She swallowed back the bile crawling up her throat. "Why do you need me now?"

He shrugged. "You're our insurance policy in case your boyfriend tries to stop us from taking off."

Hope bubbled up through the fear. If they needed insurance to make their escape, there was still a chance Jeff could find her and arrest Sherman and his son. "Where's Sherman?"

"Making preparations."

She needed to find a way to keep them on the ground for as long as possible in order to give Jeff more time. Once they were in the air, it would be nearly impossible to capture Sherman and Aaron. Such a small plane could land almost anywhere. If she could get Aaron to untie her hands and feet, maybe she could make a break for it. But she didn't know what was beyond the confines of the hangar. "Water? Can I please have some water?"

He grunted and walked away, disappearing inside the plane.

More in control of her muscles now, she managed to scoot backward until her back rested against the side of the building. Cold from the floor and wall seeped through her clothing. She shivered and worked on the rope binding her wrists together, trying to create enough space to slip her hands out or to loosen the knot. The effort warmed her almost as much as Jeff's arms would have.

She wondered what he was doing right now. Did he know she'd been kidnapped? Or did he believe she was safe and on her way home to Utah?

Were they still in Washington? She had no

idea how long she had been unconscious or how far they'd traveled. The windows in the hangar were too high up the wall for her to see anything but cloudy sky.

The large bay door of the hangar opened. She could see trees outside but no buildings. Sherman wheeled in, followed by Emil and three other guards from the compound. Her stomach plummeted with dread. Did that mean they would be leaving soon?

Aaron appeared in the doorway of the jet with a bottle of water in his hand. He moved back inside as Emil wheeled Sherman onto the plane. A few minutes later, Aaron reappeared. He no longer carried the bottle of water. He motioned for two guards to follow him as he stalked toward her.

She was cornered, trussed up like a turkey on Christmas day, and what little hope she'd been managing to hold on to evaporated. Aaron would kill her now. They were ready to take off; they didn't need her as insurance anymore. She'd never manage to escape now.

Sorrow and resignation filled her chest,

numbing her mind and her heart. Her chin dropped to her chest.

Aaron stopped in front of her, his black-and-white tennis shoes in her line of vision. "Pick her up and bring her to the plane."

Her head snapped up. "You're taking me with you?"

His lip curled with distaste. "Sherman isn't ready to get rid of you yet."

Once again, hope surged. The two guards lifted her off the ground and half carried, half dragged her to the plane, where they unceremoniously dumped her onto one of the plush leather seats. The inside of the jet was luxurious with wood-grain accents, cream-colored leather seats and and thick, dark carpeting.

Sherman sat in the seat across from her, a blanket covering his legs. No doubt there was a pistol hidden beneath the plaid wool concealing his lower half. His wheelchair had been tucked behind the seat he occupied. He smiled benevolently at her. "Aaron thinks we should dispose of you now."

Righting herself as best she could with her hands tied behind her back, she said, "And you disagree."

"I do. You hold value."

That was encouraging. Now if only there was some way to sabotage the plane so they couldn't take off.

Aaron approached from behind her and set a bottle of water in the armrest cup holder. Thirst hit her hard and fast. She couldn't do anything about it, since her hands were still tied behind her back. "Would you mind untying me so I can drink some water?"

Sherman inclined his head and lifted the edge of the draped blanket confirming he had a gun aimed at her. She met his gaze and acknowledged his power over her with a nod.

Obviously satisfied that they understood each other, Sherman dropped the covering back into place. "Aaron, untie Dr. Cleary."

Aaron let out a huff conveying his disapproval. From his back pocket, he took out a gnarly switchblade. He popped the blade open with a soft *swoosh*. She flinched. His mouth curled; obviously he enjoyed scaring her. He yanked her close to slip the knife under the rope and, with one quick flick of his wrist, cut the tie. She brought her arms forward and suppressed a wince as her shoulders protested the mistreatment. She rubbed at the red welts on her wrists; trying to loosen the rope had not been a great idea.

Aware of Sherman's gaze on her, she grabbed the water bottle, uncapped it and took several long swigs. The lukewarm water slid down easily, quenching her thirst. "Thank you."

"I'm not a monster, Dr. Cleary," he said.

She flicked her gaze toward Aaron, who had taken a seat across from them, picking his fingernails with the tip of his switchblade. But she couldn't say the same about his son.

"Where are we going?" she asked, bringing her attention back to Sherman.

"I have a sweet little place in Bhutan," he replied.

Aaron made a disgusted noise in his throat. "But she won't get to see it."

His words sliced a ribbon of fear through her. She forced herself to stay focused on Sherman. He was the only one who could control Aaron. She had to find a way to make Sherman see that killing her wasn't a smart idea. "Bhutan doesn't have an extradition treaty with the U.S."

Sherman smiled. "That is true."

"But if you kill me, do you really think they will let you come to their country?"

"We'll dump your body out over the ocean," Aaron chimed in. "They will never know you existed."

She refused to look at him despite how much she wanted to scrape her nails over his smug face.

Sherman pressed his lips together. "Aaron, check with Emil to see how close we are to takeoff."

"Fine." Aaron stood, his head nearly touching the roof.

She watched him walk toward the cockpit. Emil sat in the pilot's seat. Apparently, he was a man of many talents.

"Don't worry, Dr. Cleary," Sherman said, drawing her attention. "Killing you isn't on the agenda."

Her heart hammered in her chest. "Then what do you plan to do with me?"

"There are men who would pay top dollar for a red-haired American woman."

Repugnance rippled over her, making her quiver. Sherman was a different kind of monster. Malicious and mean, without a moral compass differentiating right from wrong. "So you're going to move from illegal drugs to human trafficking?"

"A man has to make a living." His shrug conveyed how much he didn't care.

Randy had said Sherman had changed, becoming bitter, mean and greedy. This kind of evil was beyond anything she'd ever dealt with. She wished Jeff were here; he'd know how to handle this. He'd protect her from Sherman and his vile intent. But Jeff wasn't here. She took comfort in knowing he was safe. She would have to figure out a way to escape on her own. "How could you do that to a woman?"

"Life is cruel, Dr. Cleary," he stated. "You should understand this by now."

He was cruel. She scoffed, "Because you had some bad breaks, you're going to inflict pain on others." The man was delusional. "It won't make you feel better."

"After my sweet Katherine's death, I've found very little makes me feel better. And the one thing that took the edge off my pain is being destroyed as we speak. Thanks to you."

He blamed her for finding out about his operation. Incredible. He'd been trading in slave labor by keeping all those men captive and forcing them to work. He allowed his son to cultivate and produce toxic drugs that were harming people, and he was mad at her because she and Jeff found out. The man wasn't in touch with reality. She tightened her hold on the water bottle. The plastic crumpled slightly. She stared at the bottle, remembering the weapon Jeff had made from his empty cylinder container. Had it worked? Would it work now? Could she make a similar weapon and use it to get off this plane?

"Is there a restroom?" she asked, forcing her voice to stay even so she didn't betray the loathing she felt for him.

"Back there." Sherman tipped his chin toward the rear of the plane.

Disappointed the lavatory wasn't near the cockpit, she said, "Would you mind if I used the facilities?"

"Of course not."

She lifted her feet off the floor, showing the rope around her ankles.

"Aaron!" Sherman called.

Aaron walked out of the cockpit and stopped beside his father. "Yeah, what?"

"Untie Dr. Cleary's feet," Sherman instructed.

"Not a good idea," Aaron said.

"Just do it, Aaron," Sherman said.

Aaron once again took out his switchblade and used it to cut the ties holding her ankles together. Tessa waited until he had the knife tucked away before she stood. Aaron stiffened. She made a face at him and hurried to the restroom, taking her water bottle with her.

Once inside, she drank the rest of the water, then blew into the container the way she'd seen Jeff do before recapping the lid and twisting the two ends. A pang of longing hit her. As much as she wished all this hadn't happened and she was far away from here, she couldn't ever regret meeting Jeff.

She remembered the protective way he had shielded her and helped her through this ordeal. The way he would brush back her hair, his fingers lingering on her cheek or jaw. The way he made her feel special, cared for and valued.

Determination had her squaring her shoulders and forcing back the fear that she'd never see Jeff again. She would do everything in her power to make sure she did, just as she knew he would do everything in his power to find her. She tucked the bottle inside her jacket and splashed tap water on her face. Her pale reflection stared back at her through the mirror.

"Dear Lord, please show Jeff how to find me. Let me see him again. Please. Help me out of this situation," she whispered.

She wanted to bargain with God, tell Him she'd do whatever He wanted if she could only be set free. But she knew bargaining with God wasn't the way to win His favor. His grace was hers for the asking. She had to trust Him, give every part of her life to Him despite the circumstances. If she couldn't do that, what good was faith?

*God would expect me to be smart and take action,* Jeff had said.

And so would Tessa. Lifting her chin in resolve and purpose, she went to face her enemy.

Jeff let out a growl of frustration. He stood in the middle of Henry Roscha's sparse living room. A thorough search of the house had yielded nothing. There was little furniture in the cabin, most of it homemade. A shed on the side of the cabin had also been searched and revealed all the equipment necessary for carpentry but no clues as to where Sherman and Aaron had taken Tessa.

He had to find her. If anything happened to her…He shut the thought down. He would not go there.

The dogs had quieted but now were frantically barking again.

The front door burst open. A white-haired man stood in the doorway with a shotgun aimed at Jeff's chest. "What are you doing in my home?"

"Thank you, God," Jeff murmured while raising his hands. "Are you Henry Roscha?"

"I am," Henry said, his eyes narrowed. "You're that border guy that went off with the fish lady."

"I am," Jeff said. The two tactical team members appeared with their weapons aimed at Henry. He needed Henry's cooperation. Jeff motioned them back. They kept a distance but both men kept their weapons trained on Henry. "I need your help finding Sherman."

"Why should I help you?" Henry's finger caressed the trigger. "You shot my nephew and left him to die by the stream."

Surprised, Jeff vehemently shook his head. "No, that's not how it went down. Aaron shot Randy."

Henry's lips twisted. "Aaron wouldn't hurt his own cousin."

"You were in Newhalem. Didn't you talk to Randy?"

"He was too heavily guarded," Henry said. "I couldn't get in to see him before they put him in an ambulance and took him off somewhere."

"Listen to me." Jeff needed this man to understand. "I don't have time to quibble with you. Randy helped Dr. Cleary and me escape from Sherman's compound. Aaron shot him. Now Aaron has kidnapped Dr. Cleary. I have to find her before he harms her." The thought of her hurt or worse tore Jeff up inside.

"I don't believe you. Sherman said you gunned down Randy," Henry shot back.

"You can ask Randy himself when he gets

out of surgery," Jeff said. "But by then it might be too late for Tessa. Please, we have to find her." A thread of desperation wound through his voice. "Where would your brother go? Where would he take her?"

"Why should I help you?"

"It's the right thing to do," Jeff said. Desperation made him add, "Because Randy helped us."

For a tense moment, Jeff was afraid Henry wouldn't relent. Then he slowly removed his finger from the trigger and lowered the shotgun. "I knew one day Sherman and his illegal activities would bring shame to this family."

Jeff refrained from pointing out that Henry was guilty of accessory by allowing Sherman to use his dogs and for not turning in his brother. "He's on the run. Where would he go?"

"He has property outside of the country. His safety net, he calls it. Some strange-named country with no extradition."

"All the airports, shipyards, train yards and roadways are crawling with agents looking for him and Aaron. There has to be a place where he'd lie low until he thought it safe."

Henry stroked his chin. "He keeps a jet in a hangar at Mears Field."

Jeff's stomach sank. Fear for Tessa twisted in his heart. Aaron had kidnapped Tessa from Bellingham two hours ago. It would be an hour's drive to Mears Field from there. But a four-and-a-half-hour drive for Jeff from Glen Lake, since there was no direct route.

He needed a chopper, fast.

Because once Sherman's plane took off, it would be almost impossible to bring them down without causing injury to everyone on board. Including Tessa.

But it was total supposition on his part that Sherman and Aaron would even bring Tessa on board. What if they killed her before they ever reached the plane?

All sorts of horrible scenarios played through his head, making his blood boil and fear bubble. Her lifeless body could be lying in a ditch or shallow grave along the highway. It could be days or more before she was found.

Standing here awfulizing, as his mother would say, wouldn't help him find Tessa.

"Take him into custody," Jeff said to the

tact team. While they cuffed Henry, Jeff called Coleman and filled him in. "I need a chopper to take me to Mears Field stat. And call the airport tower and tell them to ground all planes."

Not that Jeff expected Sherman to comply. But it might buy Jeff enough time to get there.

Tessa stood in the aisle of the sleek jet, thankful they weren't in the air yet. She sought to come up with a plausible excuse to move closer to the open door. She held the makeshift weapon she'd made out of the empty water bottle against her side beneath her jacket. Even if she could make it out of the plane, she would still have to contend with the guards on the ground.

*Let's deal with one obstacle at a time.*

"I've never been in an aircraft like this," she said aloud to Sherman, who was now reading a magazine. "Could I take a peek at the cockpit?"

He waved a hand, apparently too engrossed in his reading material to bother with her anymore. His overconfidence in her vulnerability worked to her advantage. "Ask Aaron."

Her insides twisted with distaste. Aaron barred the open exit. He stood on the metal frame facing outward, talking to one of the guards at the bottom of the ramp. One good shove could send him out of the plane.

Then what? Sherman had a gun. And she was sure Emil did, as well. But she'd rather die fighting than submissively comply with Sherman. Aaron had underestimated her once. Hopefully, he was arrogant enough to do so again.

Praying Aaron couldn't see her in his peripheral vision, she took a cautious step forward and noticed the coatrack full of wooden hangers right next to her. Carefully, she took a hanger off the rod and tested its weight. She could do some damage with it, so she tucked the hanger under her other arm.

Gathering her courage, she put one hand inside her jacket around the bottle and slipped the homemade weapon closer to the hem so she had better access for when she needed to use it.

She glanced back to make sure Sherman was still preoccupied. His graying head was bent slightly forward so he could read the magazine on his lap.

Inside the cockpit, Emil had his back to her, as well, while he fiddled with buttons and levers.

Aaron hadn't noticed her approach yet. Drawing strength from the adrenaline pumping through her veins, she moved in and rammed into him with her whole body, sending him tumbling completely out the plane door.

Ignoring Aaron's surprised shout, she rushed into the cockpit as Emil turned his stunned gaze on her. Aiming the bottle at his face, she quickly loosened the cap. With a pop, the white plastic lid flew off, hitting him between the eyes. He yelped with pain. The distraction gave her time to slam the cockpit door shut and throw the latch. They were locked inside.

She saw the gun lying on the copilot's seat. Emil recovered enough to leap for the weapon.

Using the hanger like a hammer, she pounded on him with all her strength. His hands came up to defend against her blows.

While still banging the wooden hanger over his head with both hands, she maneuvered herself into the copilot's seat and sat on the weapon. She reached beneath her and brought the gun up, aiming at his forehead.

Bloodied and bruised, he raised his hands in the air.

Aaron battered on the locked door, cursing and screaming. His palpable anger seeped through the barrier, making the hairs on her arms stand at attention. She was thankful he couldn't get in. He'd kill her without hesitation.

"Use the radio and call the authorities," she instructed Emil, pleased at how calm she sounded, considering she was unsteady inside.

Emil didn't move. His gaze slid from her to stare out the plane's front window. His eyes widened.

Tessa risked a glance. Men dressed in black with automatic weapons filed inside the hangar. Her hopes rose. Jeff.

There were shouts. Gunfire. More shouting. Then eerie silence. The minutes stretched. Had the good guys won? Or was her life still in danger from the men outside the cockpit door? And what of Jeff?

A knock made her jump.

"Tessa!"

She blinked. "Jeff?" A gush of relief made her hands tremble. Keeping the gun aimed at Emil, she unlatched the door and jumped back just in case her mind was playing tricks on her.

Jeff filled the doorway.

Tension oozed out of her, making her tremble as love and affection filled her soul. God had answered her prayers. Her heart, her soul, rejoiced.

"Honey, give me the gun," Jeff said.

Realizing she had the weapon aimed at him, she lowered the barrel and let him take the gun from her trembling hands. With a little gasp, she flung her arms around him. "You're really here."

The relief and tenderness on his face made her heart skip a beat.

"Sir." An officer behind Jeff gestured toward Emil, slumped in his seat and looking resigned to his fate.

Jeff led her out of the plane so the officer could take Emil into custody.

With satisfaction she saw that Sherman sat in his wheelchair, the blanket and gun gone, his hands in cuffs resting on his thighs. They'd put a stop to him once and for all. No longer would he be able to grow and sell illegal marijuana or make money off the suffering of others. A win for the good guys.

Then her gaze landed on Aaron. He knelt next to the two guards, their hands all bound with white zip ties behind their backs. He was going to jail for a very long time. Elation bubbled up in her chest. She pumped her fist. "Yes!"

Jeff's deep rumbling laugh made her giggle as the last of the tension left her body. Her knees wobbled. Jeff handed the gun to an agent and then tucked her into his side, the gesture both comforting and familiar. By his side, a place she willingly would stay for the rest of her life.

She could only pray he felt the same way, but she didn't get a chance to ask him as he propelled her toward a waiting SUV. She stopped and turned into his embrace. "Don't send me away."

Cupping her cheek in his big, strong hand, he said, "It's only for a little while. I need to see this through."

"You promise?"

He dipped his head and kissed her. A tender promise. Did she dare hope that meant he cared for her? She prayed he could love her.

He opened the door. Agent Tremont sat at the wheel. She was relieved to see him alive and in one piece.

He saluted her as she climbed in. "Dr. Cleary, I'm sorry I failed you before. It won't happen again."

She waved him off. "I'm sorry you had to suffer on my account."

"I'll see you soon." Before Jeff closed the door, he said, "I promise."

Two evenings later, Jeff stood outside Tessa's hotel room door in Seattle. His palms grew damp with nervous anxiousness. He was finally going to see her.

She'd asked to be taken to the more metropolitan city rather than back to Bellingham.

Jeff had wanted to come sooner, but they both had to give their statements, and Jeff had so much red tape to sort through that it had taken a full two days. With no immediate threats to the country that needed his attention, he'd hightailed it here to fulfill his promise. The first of many promises he planned to make to Tessa, if'd she let him.

He'd showered, shaved and changed into fresh slacks and a dress shirt beneath a wool coat. He held a dozen red long-stemmed roses in one hand. Tonight he was going to declare his love. He prayed Tessa felt the same way.

The danger to her had been neutralized— Sherman, Aaron and the others were in custody on their way to a detention facility. They would never harm Tessa or anyone else ever again. She was free to decide her future. With or without him.

He prayed with everything in him she'd choose to have a life with him.

She was an amazing woman, and he wanted to spend every moment with her. Jeff shook his head and wondered why he was surprised that Tessa had been so resourceful at taking care of herself. Independent, self-reliant and self-assured. These were words that described her. But also caring, compassionate, loyal and brave.

She was everything he'd ever want in a woman. For her alone would he risk opening his heart.

Having almost lost her, he knew that if he didn't confess his love and fight for a future with her, he'd regret it for the rest of his life. Safe wasn't what he wanted anymore. He wanted messy commitment, full of love and laughter and light. Full of Tessa.

He lifted his hand to knock just as the door flew open.

Tessa. His breath caught. She wore a silky emerald-colored dress that was modest yet clung to her curves like the garment had been handmade for her. Heeled pumps emphasized her pretty legs. And her auburn hair had been gathered up in back by a fancy clip.

His fingers twitched with the urge to undo the hair doodad and tangle in the mass of curls. She had a touch of makeup on, enough to enhance her pretty features, not hide them. He held out the flowers.

She took them and buried her nose in the

soft petals. "I was afraid you'd change your mind and not knock."

Regret for making her doubt him tugged at his conscience. Apparently, she'd been watching out the window, waiting for him to arrive. "I'm sorry." How did he explain his struggle with the fear that she'd reject him? "Are you ready?"

"Let me grab my coat and purse," she said and disappeared from view. A moment later, she reappeared in a black knee-length belted coat over her dress and a small purse clutched in her hand.

She kept the flowers with her, pressing them against her chest like a shield. Were her nerves as tied in knots as his? He hoped that would prove to be a good thing.

They made small talk on the cab ride to the Space Needle and took the elevator to the SkyCity Restaurant. They were seated at a table near the window, where the rotating panoramic view of the Emerald City, Elliott Bay and the distant mountains could be fully enjoyed. Jeff barely noticed.

Candlelight flickered from a votive on the table and deepened the contours of Tessa's pretty face. He had trouble taking his eyes off her to read the menu. She ordered Alaskan halibut. Jeff ordered something with beef and scarcely paid attention to his selection. His nerves stretched taut with the effort to contain the feelings wanting to burst from his chest.

Somehow, they made it through the meal with more small talk and shared laughs. One day he would remember what the conversation consisted of, but at the moment all he could think about was telling Tessa he loved her.

"Our meal comes with a free admittance to the observation deck. You game?" he asked her as they left the restaurant.

"I'd like that," she murmured, once again clutching the flowers in front of her.

They rode the elevator to the top of the Needle and stepped outside onto the deck. With his hand to the small of her back, they strolled along, taking in the view from five hundred and twenty feet in the air. The moon rose high in the night sky, throwing shafts of light on the Pacific Ocean. Spying a bench, he tugged her over. The crisp night air filled his lungs, bolstering his resolve.

She turned to face him. "Jeff, I—"

He cut her off with a finger to her lips. Then he sank down on one knee and took her hand. "Tessa, I love you," he blurted out.

Her eyes widened. "You do? I thought you didn't believe in love."

"I didn't think I did until you came into my life." He cupped her cheek with a hand. "I know we haven't known each other long. The past week has been intense, and our emotions were running high, but I know what is in my heart. I never expected to fall in love with you. But I did. What I feel for you is amazing. It's nothing I've ever felt for anyone else. Ever. I want a future with you. I'm one hundred percent committed to doing whatever I can to make you happy. I think you care for me. I hope—"

She put her fingertips against his lips. With eyes full of tender affection, she said, "Jeff, I love you, too."

"Really?" He had prayed and hoped so, and to hear the words coming from her sent his pulse racing.

"Really." She placed her hand over his heart. "These past few days have made me see how alone I was and how much I was missing because I was afraid of being hurt, of not being enough for anyone."

"You're more than enough for me."

Her teeth tugged on her bottom lip. Her troubled gaze held his. "What about my career?"

Memories of what she'd told him about her ex-fiancé rushed in. And his reaction. He'd been so shortsighted. He tucked a stray curl behind her ear and caressed her cheek. "I could never stand in the way of what you love to do. You've proven you're capable of anything you set your mind to. All I want is your happiness."

She sighed softly. "You do make me happy."

"I don't deserve your love, but I'm elated to know you love me." With his heart filled to the brim with love for her, he rose to sit beside her and slipped an arm around her waist, pulling her close. "I've felt the same way. Alone and lonely, scared and guarded." He eased back to look into her lovely eyes. "But with you, I'm not afraid. You have my heart."

The joy on her face set his heart pounding. She set the roses aside and turned fully into his arms. "You have my heart. I trust you completely."

Happiness exploded in his chest.

Cupping his face in her slender, capable hands, she said, "Kiss me, Agent Steele."

He arched a playful eyebrow. "Is that an order, Dr. Cleary?"

"Yes." She tugged him closer. "Please."

How could he refuse? He couldn't. As he captured her lips with his own, he sent up a silent shout of praise to God above for all the joy and love and faith that he knew would be a part of his and Tessa's life. Forever.

\* \* \* \* \*

Dear Reader,

I hope you enjoyed the first book in the Northern Border Patrol series. I'm really excited to learn and write about the men and women who keep our country safe. Thank you for coming along on Tessa and Jeff's adventures through the North Cascades National Forest. I love the setting of the Pacific Northwest. Of course, I'm a bit partial, since I reside in this beautiful part of the country.

When I was brainstorming ideas, I wanted to give Tessa a unique job, so I searched the USDA website and found the Fish and Aquatic Ecology Unit. A fish biologist sounded like a fascinating career. Pairing Tessa up with Jeff felt right from the beginning. These two had some issues to overcome as well as enemies to battle, but ultimately they triumphed.

My next book, part of the Capitol K-9 Unit continuity series from Love Inspired Suspense, comes out April 2015. Stay tuned for more Northern Border Patrol books in the coming months.

May God bless you always,

# Questions for Discussion

1. What made you pick up this book to read? In what ways did it live up to your expectations?

2. In what ways were Jeff and Tessa realistic characters? How did their romance build believably?

3. What about the setting was clear and appealing? Could you "see" where the story took place?

4. Tessa believed she worked better alone, but by the end of the story realized the value of having a partner. Do you ever find yourself in circumstances where you need to rely on a partner? Can you talk about how that worked for you?

5. Tessa guarded her heart from others because of the pain in her past. Can you talk about times in your own life that have made you want to guard your heart?

6. At the start of the book, Tessa's faith was barely there. What lessons did she learn from Jeff to help her trust God?

7. Jeff was afraid to give his heart away. Can you discuss why that was? Can you share an experience that left you feeling hurt and unwilling to open your heart?

8. Do you believe that circumstances shouldn't dictate our faith? Can you share a time when you let the circumstances of your life influence your faith?

9. Jeff's first impression of Tessa was not favorable. He made assumptions that proved false. Can you share a time when your first impression of someone turned out to be wrong?

10. Tessa came prepared for wilderness with her bag of essentials. Have you ever spent time in the wilds of a forest? If so, can you share what that experience was like?

11. Were the secondary characters believable? Did they add to the story? If so, in what ways?

12. Did you notice the Scripture in the beginning of the book? What do you think God means by these words? What application does the Scripture have to your life?

13. How did the author's use of language/writing style make this an enjoyable read?

14. Would you read more from this author? If so, why? Or why not?

15. What will be your most vivid memories of this book? Of the whole series?

# LARGER-PRINT BOOKS!

## GET 2 FREE LARGER-PRINT NOVELS PLUS 2 FREE MYSTERY GIFTS

*Love Inspired*

### Larger-print novels are now available...

# REQUEST YOUR FREE BOOKS!
## 2 FREE WHOLESOME ROMANCE NOVELS
## IN LARGER PRINT
## PLUS 2
## FREE
## MYSTERY GIFTS

**HEARTWARMING**™

*Wholesome, tender romances*

**YES!** Please send me 2 FREE Harlequin® Heartwarming Larger-Print novels and my 2 FREE mystery gifts (gifts worth about $10). After receiving them, if I don't wish to receive any more books, I can return the shipping statement marked "cancel." If I don't cancel, I will receive 4 brand-new larger-print novels every month and be billed just $4.99 per book in the U.S. or $5.74 per book in Canada. That's a savings of at least 23% off the cover price. It's quite a bargain! Shipping and handling is just 50¢ per book in the U.S. and 75¢ per book in Canada.* I understand that accepting the 2 free books and gifts places me under no obligation to buy anything. I can always return a shipment and cancel at any time. Even if I never buy another book, the two free books and gifts are mine to keep forever.

161/361 IDN F47N

| | |
|---|---|
| Name | (PLEASE PRINT) |

| | |
|---|---|
| Address | Apt. # |

| | | |
|---|---|---|
| City | State/Prov. | Zip/Postal Code |

Signature (if under 18, a parent or guardian must sign)

### Mail to the **Harlequin® Reader Service:**
**IN U.S.A.:** P.O. Box 1867, Buffalo, NY 14240-1867
**IN CANADA:** P.O. Box 609, Fort Erie, Ontario L2A 5X3

\* Terms and prices subject to change without notice. Prices do not include applicable taxes. Sales tax applicable in N.Y. Canadian residents will be charged applicable taxes. Offer not valid in Quebec. This offer is limited to one order per household. Not valid for current subscribers to Harlequin Heartwarming larger-print books. All orders subject to credit approval. Credit or debit balances in a customer's account(s) may be offset by any other outstanding balance owed by or to the customer. Please allow 4 to 6 weeks for delivery. Offer available while quantities last.

**Your Privacy**—The Harlequin® Reader Service is committed to protecting your privacy. Our Privacy Policy is available online at www.ReaderService.com or upon request from the Harlequin Reader Service.

We make a portion of our mailing list available to reputable third parties that offer products we believe may interest you. If you prefer that we not exchange your name with third parties, or if you wish to clarify or modify your communication preferences, please visit us at www.ReaderService.com/consumerschoice or write to us at Harlequin Reader Service Preference Service, P.O. Box 9062, Buffalo, NY 14269. Include your complete name and address.

HWDIR13R